GREAT ILLUSTRATED CLASSICS

SLEEPING BEAUTY
& Other Stories

BARONET BOOKS, New York, New York

GREAT ILLUSTRATED CLASSICS

edited by
Rochelle Larkin

Contents

SLEEPING BEAUTY

A Feast for the Fairies

$\mathcal{S}$LEEPING · $\mathcal{B}$EAUTY

$\mathcal{T}$here were formerly a King and a Queen, who were so sorry that they had no children; so sorry that it cannot be expressed. They went to all the waters in the world; voyages, pilgrimages, all ways were tried, and all to no purpose.

At last, however, the Queen had a daughter. There was a very fine christening; and the Princess had for her godmothers all the fairies they could find in the whole kingdom (they found seven), that every one of them might give her a gift, as was the custom of fairies in those days. By this means the Princess had all the perfections imaginable.

After the ceremonies of the christening were over, all the company returned to the King's palace, where was prepared a great feast for the fairies. There was placed before every one of them a magnificent cover with a case of massive gold, wherein were a spoon, knife, and fork, all of pure gold set with diamonds and rubies. But as they were all sitting down at table they saw come into the hall a very old fairy, whom they had not invited, because it was about fifty years since she had been out of a certain tower, and she was believed to be either dead or enchanted.

The King ordered her a cover, but could not furnish her with a case of gold as the others, because they had only seven for the seven fairies. The old fairy fancied she was slighted, and muttered some threats between her teeth. One of the young fairies who sat by her overheard how she grumbled; and, judging that she might give the little Princess some unlucky gift, went, as soon as they rose from table, and hid herself behind the wall hangings, that she might speak last, and repair, as much as she could, the evil which the old fairy might intend.

In the meanwhile all the fairies began to give their gifts to the Princess. The youngest gave her for a gift that she should be the most beautiful person in the world; the next, that she should have the wit of an angel; the third, that she should have a wonderful grace in everything she did; the fourth, that she should dance perfectly; the fifth, that she should sing like a nightingale; and the sixth, that she should play all kinds of music to the utmost perfection.

The old fairy's turn coming next, with a head shaking more with spite than age, she said that the Princess should have her hand pierced with a spindle and die of the wound. This terrible gift made the whole company tremble, and everybody fell a-crying.

At this very instant the young fairy came out from behind the hangings, and spoke these words aloud:

"Assure yourselves, O King and Queen, that your daughter

Behind the Wall Hangings

shall not die of this disaster. It is true, I have no power to undo entirely what my elder has done. The Princess shall indeed pierce her hand with a spindle; but, instead of dying, she shall only fall into a profound sleep, which shall last a hundred years, at the expiration of which a King's son shall come and awake her."

The King, to avoid the misfortune foretold by the old fairy, immediately caused a proclamation to be made, whereby everybody was forbidden, on pain of death, to spin with a distaff and spindle, or to have so much as any spindle in their houses.

About fifteen or sixteen years later, the King and Queen being gone to one of their other castles, the young Princess happened one day to divert herself by running up and down the palace; when going up from one apartment to another, she came into a little room on the top of the tower, where a good old woman, alone, was spinning with her spindle. This good woman had never heard of the King's proclamation against spindles.

"What are you doing there, goody?" said the Princess.

"I am spinning, my pretty child," said the old woman, who did not know who she was.

"Ha!" said the Princess, "this is very nice; how do you do it? Give it to me, that I may see if I can do so."

She had no sooner taken it into her hand than, whether being very hasty at it, somewhat unhandy, or that the decree of the fairy had so ordained it, it ran into her hand, and she fell down in a swoon.

"I am Spinning, My Child."

The good old woman, not knowing very well what to do in this affair, cried out for help. People came in from every quarter in great numbers; they threw water upon the Princess's face, unlaced her, struck her on the palms of her hands, and rubbed her temples with water; but nothing would bring her to herself.

And now the King, who had come back, bethought himself of the prediction of the fairies, and, judging very well that this must necessarily come to pass, since the fairies had said it, caused the Princess to be carried into the finest apartment in his palace, and to be laid upon a bed all embroidered with gold and silver.

One would have taken her for a little angel, she was so very beautiful; for her swooning away had not diminished one bit of her complexion: her cheeks were carnation, and her lips were coral; indeed her eyes were shut, but she was heard to breathe softly, which satisfied those about her that she was not dead. The King commanded that they should not disturb her, but let her sleep quietly till her hour of awaking was come.

The good fairy who had saved her life by condemning her to sleep a hundred years was in the kingdom of Matakin, twelve thousand leagues off, when this accident befell the Princess; but she was instantly informed of it by a little dwarf, who had boots of seven leagues, that is, boots with which he could tread over seven leagues of ground in one stride. The fairy came away immediately, and she arrived, about an hour after, in a fiery chariot drawn by dragons.

The King handed her out of the chariot, and she approved

A Bed All Embroidered in Silver and Gold

everything he had done; but as she had very great foresight, she thought when the Princess should awake she might not know what to do with herself, being all alone in this old palace; and this was what the good fairy did: she touched with her wand everything in the palace (except the King and the Queen) — governesses, maids of honor, ladies of the bedchamber, gentlemen, officers, stewards, cooks, undercooks, scullions, guards, pages, footmen; she likewise touched all the horses which were in the stables, the great dogs in the outward court and pretty little Mopsey too, the Princess's little spaniel, which lay by her on the bed.

Immediately upon her touching them, they all fell asleep, that they might not awake before their mistress, and that they might be ready to wait upon her when she wanted them. The very spits at the fire, as full as they could hold of partridges and pheasants, did fall asleep also. All this was done in a moment. Fairies are not long in doing their business.

And now the King and the Queen, having kissed their dear child without waking her, went out of the palace and put forth a proclamation that nobody should dare to come near it.

This, however, was not necessary, for in a quarter of an hour's time there grew up all round about the park such a vast number of trees, great and small, bushes and brambles, having one within another, that neither man nor beast could pass through; so that nothing could be seen but the very top of the towers of the palace, and then, not unless one was a good way off.

Touched with Her Wand

Nobody doubted that the fairy gave herein a very extraordinary sample of her art, that the Princess, while she continued sleeping, might have nothing to fear from any curious people.

When a hundred years were gone and passed, the son of the King then reigning, who was of another family from that of the sleeping Princess, being gone a-hunting on that side of the country, asked:

What were those towers which he saw in the middle of a great thick wood?

Everyone answered according as they had heard. Some said:

That it was a ruinous old castle, haunted by spirits;

Others: that all the sorcerers and witches of the country kept there their night's meeting.

The common opinion was that an ogre lived there, and that he carried there all the little children he could catch, that he might eat them up at his leisure, without anybody being able to follow him, as only he had the power to pass through the wood.

The Prince did not know what to believe, when a very aged countryman spoke to him thus:

"May it please your royal highness, it is now about fifty years since I heard from my father, who heard my grandfather say, that there was then in this castle a Princess, the most beautiful ever seen; that she must sleep there a hundred years, and should be awakened by a King's son, for whom she was reserved."

The young Prince was all on fire at these words, believing,

What Were Those Towers?

without weighing the matter, that he could put an end to this rare adventure; and, pushed on by love and honor, resolved that moment to look into it.

Scarce had he advanced towards the wood when all the great trees, the bushes, and brambles gave way of themselves to let him pass through; he walked up to the castle which he saw at the end of a large avenue and he entered it. What surprised him was that he saw none of his people could follow him, because the trees closed again as soon as he had passed through them. However, he did not cease from continuing his way; a young and gallant Prince is always valiant.

He came into a spacious outward court, where everything he saw might have frozen up the most fearless person with horror. There reigned over all a most frightful silence, with nothing to be seen but stretched out bodies of men and animals, all seeming to be dead. He, however, very well knew that they were only asleep; and their goblets, in which still remained some drops of wine, showed plainly that they fell asleep as they drank.

He then crossed a court paved with marble, went up the stairs, and came into the guard chamber, where guards were standing in their ranks, with their muskets upon their shoulders, and snoring as loud as they could.

After that he went through several rooms full of gentlemen and ladies, all asleep, some standing, others sitting.

At last he came into a chamber outfitted with gold and silver,

Pushed On By Love and Honor

where he saw upon a bed, the curtains of which were all open, the finest sight was ever beheld — a Princess, whose bright and, in a manner, resplendent beauty seemed somewhat divine. He approached with trembling and admiration, and fell down before her upon his knees.

And now, as the enchantment was at an end, the Princess awoke, and looking on him with eyes more tender than imaginable, asked:

"Is it you, my Prince? You have waited a long while."

The Prince, charmed with these words, and much more with the manner in which they were spoken, knew not how to show his joy and gratitude; he assured her that he loved her better than he did himself; their discourse was not well connected, they did weep more than talk — little eloquence, but a great deal of love.

He was more at a loss than she, and we need not wonder at it: she had time to think on what to say to him; for it is very probable (though history mentions nothing of it) that the good fairy, during so long a sleep, had given her very agreeable dreams. In short, they talked four hours together, and yet they said not half what they had to say.

In the meanwhile all the palace awoke; everyone thought upon their particular business, and as all of them were not in love, they were ready to die of hunger. The chief lady of honor, being as sharp set as other folks, grew very impatient, and told the Princess aloud that supper was served.

"You Have Waited a Long Time."

The Prince helped the Princess to rise; she was dressed very magnificently, but his royal highness took care not to tell her that she was dressed like his great grandmother; she looked not a bit the less charming and beautiful for all that.

They went into the great hall of mirrors, where they supped, and were served by the Princess's officers; the violins and oboes played old tunes, but very excellent, though it was now a hundred years since they had played; and after supper, without losing any time, the lord almoner married them in the chapel of the castle, and they lived happily together, perhaps even for another hundred years!

For Another Hundred Years!

The Old Shoemaker

THE · ELVES · AND · THE · SHOEMAKER

From the Brothers Grimm

There was once a shoemaker, who, through no fault of his own, became so poor that at last he had nothing left but just enough leather to make one pair of shoes. He cut out the shoes at night, so as to set to work upon them next morning; and as he had a good conscience, he laid himself quietly down in his bed and fell asleep. In the morning, after he had said his prayers, and was going to get to work, he found the pair of shoes made and finished, and standing on his table. He was very much astonished, and could not tell what to think, and he took the shoes in his hand to examine them more clearly; they were so well made that every stitch was in its right place, just as if they had come from the hand of a master-workman.

Soon after, a purchaser entered, and as the shoes fitted him very well, he gave more than the usual price for them, so that the

shoemaker had enough money to buy leather for two more pairs
of shoes. He cut them out at night, and intended to set to work
the next morning with fresh spirit; but that was not to be, for
when he got up they were already finished, and a customer even
gave him so much money that he was able to buy leather enough
for four new pairs. Early next morning he found the four pairs also
finished, and so it always happened; whatever he cut out in the
evening was worked up by the morning, so that he was soon making a good living, and in the end became very well to do.

One night, not long before Christmas, when the shoemaker
had finished cutting out, and before he went to bed, he said to his
wife,

"How would it be if we were to sit up tonight and see who it
is that does us this service?"

His wife agreed, and set a light to burn. Then they both hid
in a corner of the room, behind some coats that were hanging up,
and they began to watch. As soon as it was midnight they saw
come in two neatly formed little men, who seated themselves before the shoemaker's table, and took up the work that was already
prepared, and began to stitch, to pierce, and to hammer so clever-
ly and quickly with their little fingers that the shoemaker's eyes
could scarcely follow them, so full of wonder was he. And they
never left off until everything was finished and was standing ready
on the table, and then they jumped up and ran off.

The next morning the shoemaker's wife said to her husband,

"Spruce and Dandy Boys Are We!"

"Those little men have made us rich, and we ought to show ourselves grateful. With all their running about, and having little to cover them, they must be very cold. I'll tell you what: I will make little shirts, coats, waistcoats, and breeches for them, and knit each of them a pair of stockings, and you shall make each of them a pair of shoes."

The husband consented willingly, and at night, when everything was finished, they laid the gifts together on the table, instead of the cut-out works, and placed themselves so that they could observe how the little men would behave. When midnight came, they rushed in, ready to set to work, but when they found, instead of the pieces of prepared leather, the neat little garments ready for them, they stood a moment in surprise, and then they showed the greatest delight.

With great swiftness they took up the pretty garments and slipped them on, singing:

"What spruce and dandy boys are we!
No longer cobblers we will be."

Then they hopped and danced about, jumping over the chairs and tables, and at last they danced out the door.

From that time they were never seen again; but it always went well with the shoemaker as long as he lived, and whatever he took in hand prospered.

Whatever he Took in Hand Prospered.

"Please Spare My Home."

The · Three · Wishes

Once upon a time in a deep, dark forest there lived a poor woodsman and his wife. Every day the woodsman went out to cut down trees to make timber, and every day the work became more difficult to do.

Early one morning, after his wife had packed a meager lunch for him to take along, the woodsman started off. He went deep, deep into the forest, looking for a tree to provide him with a goodly amount of wood.

At last he spotted a great oak tree. This will make a fine day's work for me, thought the woodsman. He took his ax in both hands, swinging it over his head as he prepared to chop down the tree.

But as the ax began to descend, he heard a small voice that seemed to come from within the tree itself.

The woodsman paused in amazement, the ax stopped in mid-air. "Please, please, sir," came the voice, "do not cut down this tree, kind woodsman, please spare me my home."

The woodsman's wonder grew as from out of the very tree

itself there appeared a beautiful little spirit, standing in front of him.

The spirit repeated its plea and the woodsman, dumbfounded, at last nodded his head in agreement.

"I will do as you wish, little spirit," he said slowly, "even though it means the loss to me of a good day's work and wages."

"In doing goodness to me, I will do more than goodness to you," replied the spirit. "To show you how appreciative I am of your goodness and kindness, I will make magic for you. I will grant you the fulfillment of your next three wishes, whatsoever it may be that you wish for."

The spirit rose in the air slightly, its wings hovering, as it reached out its hand to touch the woodsman on both his shoulders. "Go now, kind man, and make your wishes with care and good thought."

The spirit disappeared, almost melting into the air, as mysteriously as it had come. The woodsman stood still for a few minutes, thoroughly dazed by all he had seen and heard. At last he recovered his senses, gathered his belongings about him, and started off through the forest for home.

As he trudged on home, his mind was full of the wonderful events of the day. He rubbed his head, wondering whether he had really seen the spirit of the tree, or if it had been a vision, or perhaps even just a dream.

All of this thinking and questioning was far more thought than he was used to, and by the time the poor woodsman found

"Make Your Wishes with Care."

himself at his own doorstep, he was thoroughly exhausted.

He went inside, wanting nothing but the comfort of his wife, his fire, and a good hot dinner.

"My, but you're home much too early for dinner to be done!" exclaimed his wife. "It lacks a good two hours before the food will be ready."

"Ah me, I wish I had a good sausage right now!" he replied.

All at once, right in front of the woodsman appeared a platter in which was sizzling as brown and perfect a sausage as he or anybody else in the world could wish for.

"How now! What is this?" asked his wife, rushing over as the fragrance of the spicy meat filled all the corners of their little house. "Where in the world did it come from?" she asked again in amazement.

It was then that the poor woodsman remembered his meeting with the spirit of the tree, and the magic that granted him his first three wishes.

"What have I done, what have I done?" the poor man groaned, holding his head in his fists. "I'd completely forgotten, and now one of my magic wishes is wasted!"

"What magic? What wishes?" his wife demanded, not understanding any of it.

It was then that he collected his senses, remembering it all, and telling her everything that had happened that afternoon.

The wife listened quietly at first, scarcely believing her ears.

"Good Sausage Right Now!"

But when she realized that one wish had already been wasted on the foolish sausage, her anger knew no limits.

"What have you done, what have you done?" she wailed over and over again, standing over her husband, waving her arms about as though she were going to strike him. "Look at this stupid sausage!" she exclaimed. "This is what you wished for when you might have gotten us all of the gold we could ever need for the rest of our lives, or a fine new house instead of this poor shack, or a coach and horses to drive us back and forth from the town whenever we wished?"

"I know, I know," the old man moaned, "but I was so hungry, all I could think of was something to eat. That's why I asked for the sausage."

"Sausage! Sausage indeed!" his wife shouted. "I wish the sausage was hanging from the tip of your nose right now!"

No sooner had the words left her mouth than the sausage, as if it could fly, rose up from the platter and attached itself exactly where she had wished it to be.

"Oh no, wife, oh no!" the old man cried. "Now look at what you've done!"

He started tugging at the sausage, trying to get it loose, but it was no use. Even when his wife added her hands to his, they could not move the sausage, not even a fraction of an inch.

The man looked up at his wife. "You know what it will take to remove it," he said, pleading with his voice and his eyes. "You

"From the Tip of Your Nose!"

know there will be only one way."

The wife bit her lip, and nodded. It was clear to both of them that only the third wish would be strong enough to remove the sausage from the end of the poor woodsman's nose.

The wife cocked her head, looking sharply at her husband. "You know," she said slowly, staring at him all the while, "if you look at it from a certain angle, it really doesn't look so bad at all. I warrant you would get used to it in very little time."

"Oh no, wife!" exclaimed the woodsman. "You can't be thinking that! You can't be wanting me to stay like this for the rest of my life!"

"You could get used to it," his wife said insistently. "Many folk have had to put up with much worse."

The poor man was beside himself. He knew that his wife wanted to save the third wish for one of her grand ideas. But what good would all that grandness be to him, he thought, if he were to spend the rest of his life in such a condition?

With all the strength he could summon, the poor woodsman shouted, "I wish this terrible thing was off my nose!"

Quick as a wink, there was the sausage once more, sizzling in the platter and sending forth the most delicious fragrances.

So there were no bags of gold, no horse-drawn carriages, no lofty palace for the poor woodsman and his wife. But, at least, for the day's adventure, they sat down to as fine a meal as had ever been served them!

Not That Bad from a Certain Angle

"Fill It at the Well of the World's End."

THE · WELL · OF · THE · WORLD'S · END

O nce upon a time, and a very good time it was, though it wasn't in my time, nor in your time, nor any one else's time, there was a girl whose mother had died, and her father had married again. And her stepmother hated her because she was more beautiful than herself, and she was very cruel to her. She used to make her do all the servant's work, and never let her have any peace.

At last, one day, the stepmother thought to get rid of her altogether; she handed her a sieve and said to her, "Go, fill it at the Well of the World's End and bring it home to me full, or woe betide you." For she thought she would never be able to find the Well of the World's End, and, if she did, how could she bring home a sieve full of water?

Well, the girl started off, and asked every one she met to tell her where was the Well of the World's End. But nobody knew, and she didn't know what to do, when a queer little old woman, all bent double, told her where it was, and how she could get to it.

So she did what the old woman told her, and at last arrived at the Well of the World's End. But when she dipped the sieve in the cold, cold water, it all ran out again. She tried and she tried again, but every time it was the same; and at last she sat down and cried as if her heart would break.

Suddenly she heard a croaking voice, and she looked up and saw a great frog with goggle eyes looking at her and speaking to her.

"What's the matter, dearie?" it asked.

"Oh, dear, oh dear," she said, "my stepmother has sent me all this long way to fill this sieve with water from the Well of the World's End, and I can't fill it at all."

"Well," said the frog, "if you promise me to do whatever I bid you for a whole night long, I'll tell you how to fill it."

So the girl agreed, and then the frog said:

"Stop it with moss and daub it with clay,
And then it will carry the water away;"

and then it gave a hop, skip and jump, and went flop into the Well of the World's End.

So the girl looked about for some moss, and lined the bottom of the sieve with it, and over that she put some clay, and then she dipped it once again into the Well of the World's End; and this time, the water didn't run out, and she turned to go away.

Just then the frog popped up its head out of the Well of the World's End, and said, "Remember your promise."

"If You Promise, I'll Show You."

"All right," said the girl; for thought she, "what harm can a frog do me?"

So she went back to her stepmother, and brought the sieve full of water from the Well of the World's End. The stepmother was angry as can be, but she said nothing at all.

That very evening they heard something tap tapping at the door low down, and a voice cried out:

> "Open the door, my honey, my heart,
> Open the door, my own darling;
> Mind you the words that you and I spoke,
> Down in the meadow at the World's End Well."

"Whatever can that be?" cried out the stepmother, and the girl had to tell her all about it, and what she had promised the frog.

"Girls must keep their promises," said the stepmother. "Go and open the door this instant." For she was glad the girl would have to obey a nasty frog.

So the girl went and opened the door, and there was the frog from the Well of the World's End. And it hopped, and it hopped, and it jumped, till it reached the girl, and then it said:

> "Lift me to your knee, my honey, my heart;
> Lift me to your knee, my own darling;
> Remember the words you and I spoke,
> Down in the meadow by the World's End Well."

But the girl didn't like to, till her stepmother said, "Lift it up this instant! Girls must keep their promises!"

"Lift Me to Your Knee."

So at last she lifted the frog up onto her lap, and it lay there for a time, till at last it said:

"Give me some supper, my honey, my heart,

Give me some supper, my darling;

Remember the words you and I spoke,

In the meadow by the Well of the World's End."

Well, she didn't mind doing that, so she got it a bowl of milk and bread, and fed it well. And when the frog had finished, it said:

"Go with me to bed, my honey, my heart,

Go with me to bed, my own darling;

Mind you the words you spoke to me,

Down by the cold well, so weary."

But that the girl wouldn't do, till her stepmother said, "Do what you promised, girl; girls must keep their promises. Do what you're bid, or out you go, you and that froggie."

So the girl took the frog with her to bed, and kept it as far away from her as she could. Well, just as the day was beginning to break what should the frog say but:

"Chop off my head, my honey, my heart,

Chop off my head, my own darling;

Remember the promise you made to me,

Down by the cold well, so weary."

At first the girl wouldn't, for she thought of what the frog had done for her at the Well of the World's End.

But when the frog said the words over again, she went and

"Out You Go, You and Froggie."

took an ax and chopped off its head, and lo and behold, there stood before her a handsome young Prince, who told her that he had been enchanted by a wicked spell, and he could never be un-spelled till some girl would do his bidding for a whole night, and chop off his head at the end of it.

The stepmother was surprised indeed when she found the young Prince instead of the nasty frog, and she wasn't best pleased, you may be sure, when the Prince told her that he was going to marry her stepdaughter because she had unspelled him.

But married they were, and went away to live in the castle of the King, his father, and all the stepmother had to console her was that it was all through her that her stepdaughter was married to a Prince.

There Was a Handsome Prince.

He Rode Into Town.

THE · FISH · AND · THE · RING

O nce upon a time, there was a mighty baron who was a great magician and knew everything that would come to pass. One day, when his little boy was four years old, he looked into the Book of Fate to see what would happen to him.

To his dismay, he found that his son would wed a lowly maid that had just been born in a house under the shadow of the near-by minster.

Now the Baron knew the father of the little girl was very, very poor, and he had five children already. So he called for his horse, and rode into town and passed by the other's house, and saw him sitting by the door, sad and doleful.

He dismounted and went up to him and said: "What is the matter, my good man?"

And the man said: "Well, your honor, the fact is, I've five children already, and now a sixth's come, a little lass, and where to get the bread from to fill their mouths, that's more than I can say."

"Don't be downhearted, my man," said the Baron. "If that's

your trouble, I can help you. I'll take away the last little one, and you won't have to bother about her."

"Thank you kindly, sir," said the man; and he went in and brought out the lass and gave her to the Baron, who mounted his horse and rode away with her. And when he got by the bank of the river, he threw the little thing into the river, and rode off to his castle.

But the little lass didn't sink; her clothes kept her up for a time, and she floated, and she floated, till she was cast ashore just in front of a fisherman's hut. There the fisherman found her, and took pity on the poor little thing and took her into his house, and she lived there till she was fifteen years old, and a fine handsome girl.

One day it happened that the Baron went out hunting with some companions along the banks of the river, and stopped at the fisherman's hut to get a drink and the girl came out to give it to them. They all noticed her beauty, and one of them said to the Baron: "You can read fates, Baron, whom will she marry, d'ye think ?"

"Oh! that's easy to guess," said the Baron, "some yokel or other. But I'll cast her horoscope. Come here, girl, and tell me on what day you were born."

"I don't know, sir," said the girl, "I was picked up just here after having been brought down by the river about fifteen years ago."

Then the Baron knew who she was, and when they went

She Floated Till Cast Ashore.

away, he rode back and said to the girl: "Hark ye, girl, I will make your fortune. Take this letter to my brother, and you will be settled for life." The girl took the letter and said she would go. Now this was what he had written in the letter:

"Dear Brother — Take the bearer and put her to death immediately.

"Yours affectionately,

Humphrey."

Soon after the girl set out and slept for the night at a little inn. Now that very night a band of robbers broke into the inn, and searched the girl, who had no money, but only the letter. So they opened this and read it, and thought it a shame.

The captain of the robbers took a pen and paper and wrote this letter:

"Dear Brother — Take the bearer and marry her to my son immediately.

"Yours affectionately,

Humphrey."

And then he gave it to the girl, bidding her begone. So she went on to the Baron's brother, a noble knight, with whom the Baron's son was staying. When she gave the letter to the brother, he gave orders for the wedding to be prepared at once, and they were married that very day.

Soon after, the Baron himself came to his brother's castle, and what was his surprise to find that the very thing he had plotted

"Yours Affectionately, Humphrey."

against had come to pass! But he was not to be put off that way; and he took the girl for a walk, as he said, along the cliffs. And when he got her all alone, he took her by the arms, and was going to throw her over.

But she begged hard for her life. "I have not done anything," she said, "if only you will spare me, I will do whatever you wish. I will never see you or your son again till you desire it."

Then the Baron took off his gold ring and threw it into the sea, saying: "Never let me see your face till you can show me that ring," and he let her go.

The poor girl wandered on and on, till at last she came to a great noble's castle, and she asked to have some work given to her; and they made her the scullion girl of the castle, for she had been used to such work in the fisherman's hut.

Now one day, who should she see coming up to the noble's house but the Baron, his brother, and his son, her husband. She didn't know what to do, but thought they would not see her in the castle kitchen. So she went back to her work with a sigh, and set to cleaning a huge big fish that was to be boiled for their dinner.

And, as she was cleaning it, she saw something shine inside it, and what do you think she found? Why, there was the Baron's ring, the very one he had thrown over the cliff! She was glad indeed to see it, you may be sure. Then she cooked the fish as nicely as she could, and served it up.

Well, when the fish came on the table, the guests liked it so

"Till You Can Show Me That Ring."

well that they asked the noble who cooked it. He said he didn't know, but called to his servants: "Ho, there, send the cook who cooked that fine fish." So they went down to the kitchen and told the girl she was wanted in the hall. Then she made herself ready and put the Baron's gold ring on her thumb and went up into the hall.

When the banqueters saw such a young and beautiful cook they were surprised. But the Baron was in a tower of a temper, and started up as if he would do her some violence.

The girl went up to him with her hand before her with the ring on it, and she put it down before him on the table. Then at last the Baron saw that no one could fight against Fate, and he handed her to a seat and announced to all the company that this was his son's true wife. He took her and his son home to his castle, and they all lived as happy as could be ever afterwards.

"Send the Cook Who Cooked That Fish."

Not Really a Crow

THE · BRAVE · LITTLE · PRINCESS

O nce upon a time there were three Princesses who were all
young and beautiful; but the youngest, although she was
not fairer than the other two, was the most loveable of them
all.

About half a mile from the palace in which they lived there
stood a castle, which was uninhabited and almost a ruin, but the
garden which surrounded it was a mass of blooming flowers, and
in this garden the youngest Princess often used to walk.

One day when she was pacing to and fro under the lime trees,
a black crow hopped out of a rosebush in front of her. The poor
bird was all torn and bleeding, which made the kind little Princess
quite upset. When the crow saw this it turned to her and said:

"I am not really a crow, but an enchanted Prince, who has
been doomed to spend his youth in misery. If you only liked,
Princess, you could save me. But you would have to say good-bye
to all your own people and come and be my constant companion
in this ruined castle. There is one habitable room in it, in which

there is a golden bed; there you will have to live all by yourself, and don't forget that whatever you may see or hear in the night you must not scream out, for if you give as much as a single cry my sufferings will be doubled."

The good natured Princess at once left her home and her family and hurried to the ruined castle, and took possession of the room with the golden bed.

When night approached she lay down, but though she shut her eyes tight, sleep would not come. At midnight she heard to her great horror someone coming along the passage, and in a minute her door was flung wide open and a troop of strange beings entered the room. They at once proceeded to light a fire in the huge fireplace; then they placed a great cauldron of boiling water on it. When they had done this, they approached the bed on which the trembling girl lay, and, screaming and yelling all the time, they dragged her towards the cauldron. She nearly died with fright, but she never uttered a sound. When of a sudden the cock crowed, all the evil spirits vanished.

At the same moment the crow appeared and hopped all round the room with joy. It thanked the Princess most heartily for her goodness, and said that its sufferings had already been greatly lessened.

Now one of the Princess's elder sisters, who was very inquisitive, had found out about everything, and went to pay her youngest sister a visit in the ruined castle. She implored her so urgently to let

The Room With the Golden Bed

her spend the night with her in the golden bed, that at last the good natured little Princess consented. But at midnight, when the odd folk appeared, the elder sister screamed with terror, and from this time on the youngest Princess insisted always on keeping watch alone.

So she lived in solitude all the daytime, and at night she would have been frightened, had she not been so brave; but every day the crow came and thanked her for her endurance, and assured her that his sufferings were far less than they had been.

And so two years passed away, when one day the crow came to the Princess and said: "In another year I shall be freed from the spell I am under at present, because then the seven years will be over. But before I can resume my natural form, and take possession of the belongings of my forefathers, you must go out into the world as a maidservant."

The young Princess consented at once, and for a whole year she served as a maid; but in spite of her youth and beauty she was very badly treated, and suffered many things. One evening, when she was spinning flax, and had worked her little hands weary, she heard a rustling beside her and a cry of joy. Then she saw a handsome youth standing beside her who knelt down at her feet and kissed the little weary hands.

"I am the Prince," he said, "who you in your goodness, when I was wandering about in the shape of a crow, freed from the most awful torments. Come now to my castle with me, and let us live

Every Day the Crow Thanked Her.

there happily together."

At first, the Princess was afraid; such terrible sights had she seen at that place, for the Prince's sake. Besides, it was such a ruin, how could they possibly live in just that one room with its narrow golden bed?

But the Prince insisted gently and the Princess, who did love him so much, at last consented.

So they went to the castle where they had both endured so much. But when they reached it, it was difficult to believe that it was the same, for it had all been rebuilt and done up again. And there they lived for a hundred years, a hundred years of joy and happiness.

A Hundred Years of Joy

"The Emperor is in the Wardrobe."

THE · EMPEROR'S · NEW · CLOTHES

By Hans Christian Andersen

Many years ago there lived an Emperor who was so fond of new clothes that he spent all his money on them in order to be beautifully dressed. He did not care about his soldiers, he did not care about the theater; he only liked to go out walking to show off his new clothes. He had a coat for every hour of the day; and just as they say of a King, "He is in the council-chamber," here they always said, "The Emperor is in the wardrobe."

In the great city in which he lived there was always something going on; every day many strangers came there. One day two impostors arrived who gave themselves out as weavers, and said that they knew how to manufacture the most beautiful cloth imaginable. Not only were the texture and pattern uncommonly beautiful, but the clothes which were made of the stuff possessed this wonderful property: they were invisible to anyone who was not fit for his office, or who was unpardonably stupid.

"Those must indeed be splendid clothes," thought the Emperor. "If I had them on I could find out which men in my kingdom are unfit for the offices they hold; I could distinguish the wise from the stupid! Yes, this cloth must be woven for me at once." And he gave both the impostors much money, so that they might begin their work.

They placed two weaving-looms, and began to do as if they were working, but they had not the least thing on the looms. They also demanded the finest silk and the best gold, which they put in their pockets, and "worked" at the empty looms till late into the night.

"I should like very much to know how far they have got on with the cloth," thought the Emperor. But at once he remembered that whoever was stupid or not fit for his office would not be able to see it.

Now he certainly believed that he had nothing to fear for himself, but he wanted first to send somebody else in order to see how he stood with regard to his office. Everybody in the whole town knew what a wonderful power the cloth had, and they were all curious to see how bad or how stupid their neighbor was.

"I will send my old and honored minister to the weavers," thought the Emperor. "He can judge best what the cloth is like, for he has intellect, and no one understands his office better than he."

Now the good old minister went into the hall where the two

"This Cloth Must Be Woven."

impostors sat drinking at the empty weaving-looms. "Dear me!" thought the old minister, opening his eyes wide, "I can see nothing!" But he did not say so.

Both the impostors begged him to be so kind as to step closer, and asked him if it were not a beautiful texture and lovely colors. They pointed to the empty loom, and the poor old minister went forward rubbing his eyes; but he could see nothing, for there was nothing there.

"Dear, dear!" thought he, "Can I be stupid? I have never thought that, and nobody must know it! Can I be not fit for my office? No, I must certainly not say that I cannot see the cloth!"

"Have you nothing to say about it?" asked one of the men who was weaving.

"Oh, it is lovely, most lovely!" answered the old minister, looking through his spectacles. "What a texture! What colors! Yes, I will tell the Emperor that it pleases me very much."

"Now we are delighted at that," said both the weavers, and they named the colors and explained the make of the texture.

The old minister paid great attention, so that he could tell the same to the Emperor when he came back to him, which he did.

The impostors now wanted more money, more silk, and more gold to use in their weaving. They put it all in their own pockets, and there came no threads on the loom, but they went on as they had done before at the empty loom.

The Emperor soon sent another worthy statesman to see how

"Lovely, Most Lovely!"

the weaving was getting on, and whether the cloth would soon be finished. It was the same with him as the first one; he looked and looked, but because there was nothing on the empty loom he could see nothing.

"Is it not a beautiful piece of cloth?" asked the two impostors, and they pointed to and described the splendid material which was not there.

"Stupid I am not!" thought the man, "so it must be my good office for which I am not fitted. It is strange, certainly, but no one must be allowed to notice it." And so he praised the cloth which he did not see, and expressed to them his delight at the beautiful colors and the splendid texture. "Yes, it is quite beautiful," he said to the Emperor.

Everybody in the town was talking of the magnificent cloth.

Now the Emperor wanted to see it himself while it was still on the loom. With a great crowd of select followers, amongst whom were both the worthy statesmen who had already been there before, he went to the cunning impostors, who were now weaving with all their might, but without fiber or thread.

"Is it not splendid!" said both the old statesmen who had already been there. "See, your Majesty, what a texture! What colors!" And then they pointed to the empty loom, for they believed that the others could see the cloth quite well.

"What!" thought the Emperor, "I can see nothing. This is indeed horrible! Am I stupid? Am I not fit to be Emperor? That is

"Stupid I Am Not!"

the most dreadful thing that could happen to me.

"Oh, it is very beautiful," he said out loud. "It has my gracious approval." And then he nodded pleasantly, and examined the empty loom, for he would not say that he could see nothing.

His whole court round him looked and looked, and saw no more than the others; but they said, like the Emperor, "Oh! It is beautiful!" And they advised him to wear these new and magnificent clothes for the first time at the great procession which was soon to take place. "Splendid! Lovely! Most beautiful!" went from mouth to mouth; everyone seemed delighted over them, and the Emperor gave to the impostors the title of Court Weavers to the Emperor.

Throughout the whole of the night before the morning on which the procession was to take place, the impostors were up and were working by the light of more than sixteen candles. The people could see that they were very busy making the Emperor's new clothes ready. They pretended they were taking the cloth from the loom, cut with huge scissors in the air, sewed with needles without thread, and then said at last, "Now the clothes are finished!"

The Emperor came himself with his most distinguished knights, and each impostor held up his arm just as if he were holding something, and said, "See! Here are the breeches! Here is the coat! Here the cloak!" and so on.

"Spun clothes are so comfortable that one would imagine one had nothing on at all; but that is the beauty of it!" said all the

Needles Without Thread

knights, but they could see nothing, for there was nothing there.

"Will it please your Majesty graciously to take off your clothes," said the impostors, "then we will put on the new clothes, here before the mirror."

The Emperor took off all his clothes, and the impostors placed themselves before him as if they were putting on each part of his new clothes as was ready, and the Emperor turned and bent himself in front of the mirror.

"How beautifully they fit! How well they sit!" said everybody. "What material! What colors! It is a gorgeous suit!"

"They are waiting outside with the canopy which your Majesty is to have borne over you in the procession," announced the Master of the Ceremonies.

"Look, I am ready," said the Emperor. "Doesn't it sit well!" And he turned himself again to the mirror to see if his finery was on all right.

The chamberlains who were used to carry the train put their hands near the floor as if they were lifting up the train; then they did as if they were holding something in the air. They would not have it noticed that they could see nothing.

So the Emperor went along in the procession under the splendid canopy, and all the people in the streets and at the windows said, "How matchless are the Emperor's new clothes! That train fastened to his dress, how beautifully it hangs."

No one wished it to be noticed that he could see nothing, for

"What Material! What Colors!"

then he would have been unfit for his office, or else very stupid. None of the Emperor's clothes had met with such approval as these had.

"But he has nothing on!" said a little child at last.

"Just listen to the innocent child!" said the father, and each one whispered to his neighbor what the child had said.

"But he has nothing on!" the whole of the people called out at last.

This struck the Emperor, for it seemed to him as if they were right; but he thought to himself, "I must go on with the procession now." And the chamberlains walked along still more uprightly, holding up the train which was not there at all!

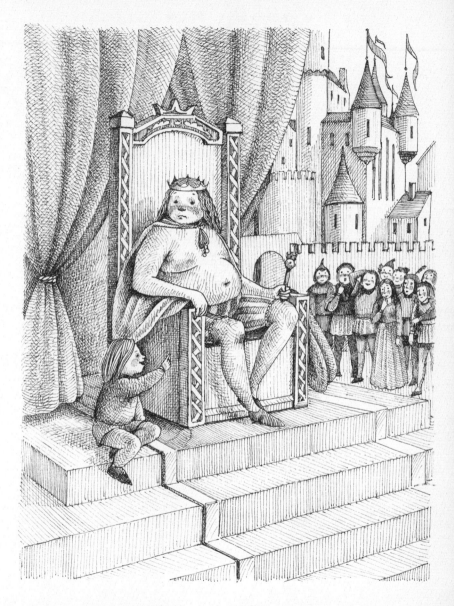

"But He Has Nothing On!"

Only One Eye and Only One Tooth

Fairer-Than-A-Fairy

O nce there lived a King who had no children for many years after his marriage. At length heaven granted him a daughter of such remarkable beauty that he could think of no name so appropriate for her as "Fairer-than-a-Fairy."

It never occurred to the good-natured monarch that such a name was certain to call down the hatred and jealousy of all the fairies on the child, but this was what happened. No sooner had they heard of this presumptuous name than they resolved to gain possession of her who bore it, and either to torment her cruelly, or at least to conceal her from the eyes of all men.

The eldest of their tribe was entrusted to carry out their revenge. This fairy was named Lagree; she was so old that she only had one eye and one tooth left, and even these poor remains she had to keep all night in a strengthening liquid. She was also so spiteful that she gladly devoted all her time to carrying out all the mean or ill-natured tricks of the whole body of fairies.

With her large experience, added to her native spite, she

found but little difficulty in carrying off Fairer-than-a-Fairy. The poor child, who was only seven years old, nearly died of fear on finding herself in the power of this hideous creature. However, when after an hour's journey underground she found herself in a splendid palace with lovely gardens, she felt a little reassured, and was further cheered when she discovered that her pet cat and dog had followed her.

The old fairy led her to a pretty room which she said should be hers, at the same time giving her the strictest orders never to let go out the fire which was burning brightly in the grate. She then gave two glass bottles into the Princess's charge, desiring her to take the greatest care of them, and having enforced her orders with the most awful threats in case of disobedience, she vanished, leaving the little girl at liberty to explore the palace and grounds and a good deal relieved at having only two apparently easy tasks set her.

Several years passed, during which time the Princess grew accustomed to her lonely life, obeyed the fairy's orders, and by degrees forgot all about the court of the King her father.

One day, whilst passing near a fountain in the garden, she noticed that the sun's rays fell on the water in such a manner as to produce a brilliant Rainbow. She stood still to admire it, when, to her great surprise, she heard a voice addressing her which seemed to come from the center of its rays. The voice was that of a young man, and its sweetness of tone and the agreeable things it uttered, led her to infer that its owner must be equally charming; but this

Her Pet Cat and Dog Had Followed Her.

had to be a mere matter of fancy, for no one was visible.

The beautiful Rainbow informed Fairer-than-a-Fairy that he was young, the son of a powerful King, and that the fairy Lagree, who owed his parents a grudge, had revenged herself by depriving him of his natural shape for some years; that she had imprisoned him in the palace, where he had found his confinement hard to bear for some time, but now, he owned, he no longer sighed for freedom since he had seen and learned to love Fairer-than-a-Fairy.

He added many other tender speeches to this declaration, and the Princess, to whom such remarks were a new experience, could not help feeling pleased and touched by his attentions.

The Prince could only appear or speak under the form of a Rainbow, and it was therefore necessary that the sun should shine on water so as to enable the rays to form themselves.

Fairer-than-a-Fairy lost no moment in which she could meet Prince Rainbow, and they enjoyed many long and interesting interviews. One day, however, their conversation became so absorbing and time passed so quickly that the Princess forgot to attend to the fire, and it went out.

Lagree, on her return, soon found out the neglect, and seemed only too pleased to have the opportunity of showing her spite to her lovely prisoner. She ordered Fairer-than-a-Fairy to start next day at dawn to ask Locrinos for fire with which to relight the one she had allowed to go out.

Now this Locrinos was a cruel monster who devoured every-

Rainbow—the Son of a King

one he came across, and especially enjoyed a chance of catching any young girls. Our heroine obeyed with great sweetness, and without having been able to take leave of her love, she set off to go to Locrinos as to certain death. As she was crossing a wood a bird said to her to pick up a shining pebble which she would find in a fountain close by, and to use it when needed. She took the bird's advice, and in due time arrived at the house of Locrinos.

Luckily she only found his wife at home, who was much struck by the Princess's youth and beauty and sweet gentle manners, and still further impressed by the present of the shining pebble.

She readily let Fairer-than-a-Fairy have the fire, and in return for the stone she gave her another, which, she said, might prove useful some day. Then she sent her away without doing her any harm.

Lagree was as much surprised as displeased at the happy result of this expedition, and Fairer-than-a-Fairy waited anxiously for an opportunity of meeting Prince Rainbow and telling him her adventures. She found, however, that he had already been told all about them by a fairy who protected him, and to whom he was related.

The dread of fresh dangers to his beloved Princess made him devise some more convenient way of meeting than by the garden fountain, and Fairer-than-a-Fairy carried out his plan daily with entire success. Every morning she placed a large basin full of water

She Took the Bird's Advice.

on her window-sill, and as soon as the sun's rays fell on the water the Rainbow appeared as clearly as it had ever done in the fountain. By this means they were able to meet without losing sight of the fire or of the two bottles in which the old Fairy kept her eye and her tooth at night, and for some time they enjoyed every hour of sunshine together.

One day Prince Rainbow appeared in the depths of woe. He had just heard that he was to be banished from this lovely spot, but he had no idea where he was to go. The poor young couple were in despair, and only parted with the last ray of sunshine, and in hopes of meeting next morning. Alas! next day was dark and gloomy, and it was only late in the afternoon that the sun broke through the clouds for a few minutes.

Fairer-than-a-Fairy eagerly ran to the window, but in her haste she upset the basin, and spilt all the water with which she had carefully filled it overnight. No other water was at hand except that in the two bottles. It was the only chance of seeing her love before they were separated, and she did not hesitate to break the bottles and pour their contents into the basin, and the Rainbow appeared at once.

Their farewells were full of tenderness; the Prince made the most ardent and sincere protestations, and promised to neglect nothing which might help to deliver his dear Fairer-than-a-Fairy from her captivity, and implored her to consent to their marriage as soon as they should both be free.

The Rainbow Appeared.

The Princess, on her side, vowed to have no other husband, and declared herself willing to brave death itself in order to rejoin him.

They were not allowed much time for their good-byes; the Rainbow vanished, and the Princess, resolved to run all risks, started off at once, taking nothing with her but her dog, her cat, a sprig of myrtle, and the stone which the wife of Locrinos gave her.

When Lagree became aware of her prisoner's flight she was furious, and set off at full speed in pursuit. She overtook her just as the poor girl, overcome by fatigue, had lain down to rest in a cave which the stone had formed to shelter her. The little dog, who was watching her mistress, promptly flew at Lagree and bit her so severely that she stumbled against a corner of the cave and broke off her only tooth. Before she had recovered from the pain and rage this caused her, the Princess had time to escape, and was some way on her road. Fear gave her strength for some time, but at last she could go no further, and sank down to rest. As she did so, the sprig of myrtle she carried touched the ground, and immediately a green and shady bower sprang up round her, in which she hoped to sleep in peace.

But Lagree had not given up her pursuit, and arrived just as Fairer-than-a-Fairy had fallen fast asleep. This time she made sure of catching her victim, but the cat spied her out, and, springing from one of the boughs of the arbor she flew at Lagree's face and tore out her only eye, thus delivering the Princess forever from her persecutor.

At Full Speed in Pursuit

One might have thought that all would now be well, but no sooner had Lagree been put to flight than our heroine was overwhelmed with hunger and thirst. She felt as though she should certainly expire, and it was with some difficulty that she dragged herself as far as a pretty little green and white house, which stood at no great distance. Here she was received by a beautiful lady dressed in green and white to match the house, which apparently belonged to her, and of which she seemed the only inhabitant.

She greeted the fainting Princess most kindly, gave her an excellent supper, and after a long night's rest in a delightful bed told her that after many troubles she would finally attain her desire.

As the green and white lady took leave of the Princess she gave her a nut, desiring her only to open it in the most urgent need.

After a long and tiring journey Fairer-than-a-Fairy was once more received in a house, and by a lady exactly like the one she had quitted. Here again she received a present with the same injunctions, but instead of a nut this lady gave her a golden pomegranate. The mournful Princess had to continue her weary way, and after many troubles and hardships she again found rest and shelter in a third house exactly like the two others.

These houses belonged to three sisters, all endowed with fairy gifts, and all so alike in mind and person that they wished their houses and garments to be equally alike. Their occupation consisted of helping those in misfortune, and they were as gentle and benevolent as Lagree had been cruel and spiteful.

Received by a Beautiful Lady

The third fairy comforted the poor traveler, begged her not to lose heart, and assured her that her troubles should be rewarded. She accompanied her advice by the gift of a crystal smelling-bottle, with strict orders to open it only in case of urgent need. Fairer-than-a-Fairy thanked her warmly, and resumed her way cheered by pleasant thoughts.

After a time her road led through a wood, full of soft airs and sweet odors, and before she had gotten a hundred yards she saw a wonderful silver castle suspended by strong silver chains to four of the largest trees. It was so perfectly hung that a gentle breeze rocked it sufficiently to send you pleasantly to sleep.

Fairer-than-a-Fairy felt a strong desire to enter this castle, but besides its being hung a little above the ground, there seemed to be neither doors nor windows. She had no doubt (though really she couldn't think why) that the moment had come in which to use the nut which had been given her. She opened it, and out came a diminutive hall porter at whose belt hung a tiny chain, at the end of which was a golden key half as long as the smallest pin you ever saw.

The Princess climbed up one of the silver chains, holding in her hand the little porter who, in spite of his minute size, opened a secret door with his golden key and let her in. She entered a magnificent room which appeared to occupy the entire castle, and which was lighted by gold and jewelled stars in the ceiling. In the midst of this room stood a couch, draped with curtains of all the colors of the rainbow, and suspended by golden cords so that it

A Wonderful Silver Castle

swayed with the castle in a manner which rocked its occupant delightfully to sleep.

On this elegant couch lay Prince Rainbow, looking more beautiful than ever, and sunk in profound slumber, in which he had been held ever since his disappearance.

Fairy-than-a-Fairy, who now saw him for the first time in his real shape, hardly dared to gaze at him, fearing his appearance might not be in keeping with the voice and language which had won her heart. At the same time she could not help feeling rather hurt at the apparent indifference with which she was received.

She related all the dangers and difficulties she had gone through, and though she repeated the story twenty times in a loud clear voice, the Prince slept on and took no heed. She then had recourse to the golden pomegranate, and on opening it found that all the seeds were little violins which flew up in the vaulted roof and at once began playing melodiously.

The Prince was not completely roused, but he opened his eyes a little and looked all the handsomer.

Impatient at not being recognized, Fairer-than-a-Fairy now drew out her third present, and on opening the crystal scent-bottle a little siren flew out, who silenced the violins and then sang close to the Prince's ear the story of all his lady love had suffered in her search for him. She added some gentle reproaches to her tale, but before she had got far he was wide awake, and, transported with joy, threw himself at the Princess's feet.

The Prince Slept On.

At the same moment the walls of the room expanded and opened out, revealing a golden throne covered with jewels. A magnificent court now began to assemble, and at the same time several elegant carriages filled with ladies in magnificent dresses drove up.

In the first and most splendid of these carriages sat Prince Rainbow's mother. She fondly embraced her son, after which she informed him that his father had been dead for some years, that the anger of the fairies was at length appeased, and that he might return in peace to reign over his people, who were longing for his presence.

The court received the new King with joyful acclamations which would have delighted him at any other time, but all his thoughts were full of Fairer-than-a-Fairy. He was just about to present her to his mother and the court, feeling sure that her charms would win all hearts, when the three sisters dressed in green and white appeared.

They declared the secret of Fairer-than-a-Fairy's royal birth, and the Queen, taking the two lovers in her carriage, set off with them for the capital of the kingdom.

Here they were received with tumultuous joy. The wedding was celebrated without delay, and succeeding years diminished not the virtues, beauty, nor the mutual affection of King Rainbow and his Queen, Fairer-than-a-Fairy.

A Magnificent Court

In Her Hands, A Little Wheel

CATHERINE · AND · HER · DESTINY

Long ago there lived a rich merchant who, besides possessing more treasures than any king in the world, had in his great hall three chairs: one of silver, one of gold, and one of diamonds. But his greatest treasure of all was his only daughter, who was called Catherine.

One day Catherine was sitting in her own room when suddenly the door flew open, and in came a tall and beautiful woman holding in her hands a little wheel.

"Catherine," she said, going up to the girl, "which would you rather have — a happy youth or a happy old age?"

Catherine was so taken by surprise that she did not know what to answer, and the lady repeated again, "Which would you rather have — a happy youth or a happy old age?"

Then Catherine thought to herself, "If I say a happy youth, then I shall have to suffer all the rest of my life. No, I would bear trouble now, and have something better to look forward to." So she looked up and replied, "Give me a happy old age."

"So be it," said the lady, and turned her wheel as she spoke, vanishing the next moment as suddenly as she had come.

Now this beautiful lady was the Destiny of poor Catherine.

Only a few days after this the merchant heard the news that all his finest ships, laden with the richest merchandise, had been sunk in a storm, and he was left a beggar. The shock was too much for him. He took to his bed, and in a short time he was dead of his disappointment.

So poor Catherine was left alone in the world without a penny or a creature to help her. But she was a brave girl and full of spirit, and soon made up her mind that the best thing she could do was to go to the nearest town and become a servant.

She lost no time in getting herself ready, and did not take long over her journey; and as she was passing down the chief street of the town a noble lady saw her out of the window, and, struck by her sad face, said to her, "Where are you going all alone, my pretty girl?"

"Ah, my lady, I am very poor, and must go to service to earn my bread."

"I will take you into my service," said she; and Catherine served her well.

Some time after her mistress said to Catherine, "I am obliged to go out for a long while, and must lock the house door, so that no thieves shall get in."

So she went away, and Catherine took her work and sat down

Left Alone in the World

at the window. Suddenly the door burst open, and in came her Destiny.

"Oh! so here you are, Catherine! Did you really think I was going to leave you in peace?" And as she spoke she walked to the linen press where Catherine's mistress kept all her finest sheets and underclothes, tore everything in pieces, and flung them on the floor.

Poor Catherine wrung her hands and wept, for she thought to herself, "When my lady comes back and sees all this ruin she will think it is my fault," and, starting up, she fled through the open door.

Then Destiny took all the pieces and made them whole again, and put them back in the press, and when everything was tidy she too left the house.

When the mistress reached home she called Catherine, but Catherine was not there. "Can she have robbed me?" thought the old lady, and looked hastily round the house; but nothing was missing. She wondered why Catherine should have disappeared like this, but she heard no more of her, and in a few days she filled her place with another girl.

Meanwhile Catherine wandered on and on, without knowing very well where she was going, till at last she came to another town. Just as before, a noble lady happened to see her passing her window, and called out to her, "Where are you going all alone, my pretty girl?"

Everything in Pieces

And Catherine answered, "Ah, my lady, I am very poor, and must go to service to earn my bread."

"I will take you into my service," said the lady; and Catherine served her well, and hoped she might now be left in peace. But, exactly as before, one day when Catherine was left in the house alone her Destiny came again and spoke to her with hard words: "What! Are you here now?"

And in a passion she tore up everything she saw, till in sheer misery poor Catherine rushed out of the house. And so it befell for seven years, and whenever Catherine found a fresh place her Destiny came and forced her to leave it.

After seven years, however, Destiny seemed to get tired of persecuting her, and a time of peace set in for Catherine.

When she had been chased away from her last house by Destiny's wicked pranks she had taken service with another lady, who told her that it would be part of her daily work to walk to a mountain that overshadowed the town, and, climbing up to the top, she was to lay on the ground some loaves of freshly baked bread, and cry with a loud voice, "O Destiny, my mistress," three times. Then her lady's Destiny would come and take away the offering.

"That will I gladly do," said Catherine.

So the years went by, and Catherine was still there, and every day she climbed the mountain with her basket of bread on her arm. She was happier than she had been, but sometimes, when no one saw her, she would weep as she thought over her old life, and

"I Must Earn My Bread."

how different it was to the one she was now leading.

One day her lady saw her, and said, "Catherine, what is it? Why are you always weeping?" And then Catherine told her story.

"I have got an idea," exclaimed the lady. "Tomorrow, when you take the bread to the mountain, you shall pray my Destiny to speak to yours, and entreat her to leave you in peace. Perhaps something may come of it!"

At these words Catherine dried her eyes, and next morning, when she climbed the mountain, she told all she had suffered, and cried, "O Destiny of my mistress, pray, I entreat you, of my Destiny that she may leave me in peace."

And this Destiny answered, "Oh, my poor girl, know you not your Destiny lies buried under seven coverlets, and can hear nothing? But if you will come tomorrow, I will bring her with me."

And after Catherine had gone her way, her lady's Destiny went to find her sister, and said to her, "Dear sister, has not Catherine suffered enough? It is surely time for her good days to begin."

The sister answered, "Tomorrow you shall bring her to me, and I will give her something that may help her out of her need."

The next morning Catherine set out earlier than usual for the mountain, and her lady's Destiny took the girl by the hand and led her to her sister Destiny, who lay under the seven coverlets. And her Destiny held out to Catherine a ball of silk, saying, "Keep this — it may be useful some day," and then pulled the coverings over her head again.

"Pray, I Entreat You, of My Destiny."

But Catherine walked sadly down the hill, and went straight to her lady and showed her the silken ball, which was the end of all her high hopes.

"What shall I do with it?" she asked. "It is not worth sixpence, and it is no good to me!"

"Take care of it," replied her mistress. "Who can tell how useful it may be?"

A little while after this, grand preparations were made for the King's marriage, and all the tailors in the town were busy embroidering fine clothes. The wedding garment was so beautiful nothing like it had ever been seen before, but when it was almost finished the tailor found that he had no more silk. The color was very rare, and none could be found like it, and the King made a proclamation that if anyone happened to possess any, they should bring it to the court, and he would give them a large sum.

"Catherine!" exclaimed the lady, who had been to the tailors and seen the wedding garment, "your ball of silk is exactly the right color. Bring it to the King, and you can ask what you like for it."

Then Catherine put on her best clothes and went to the court, and looked more beautiful than any woman there.

"May it please your majesty," she said, "I have brought you a ball of silk of the color you asked for, as no one else has any in the town."

"Your majesty," asked one of the courtiers, "shall I give the maiden its weight in gold?"

Catherine Showed Her the Silken Ball.

The King agreed, and a pair of scales were brought; and a handful of gold was placed in one scale and the silken ball in the other. But lo! Let the King lay in the scales as many gold pieces as he would, the silk was always heavier still.

Then the King took some larger scales, and heaped up all his treasures on the one side, but the silk on the other outweighed them all. At last there was only one thing left that had not been put in, and that was his golden crown. And he took it from his head and set it on top of all, and at last the scale moved and the ball had found its balance.

"Where got you this silk?" asked the King.

"It was given me, royal majesty, by my mistress," replied Catherine.

"That is not true," said the King, "and if you do not tell me the truth I will have your head off this instant."

So Catherine told him the whole story, and how she had once been as rich as he.

Now there lived at the court a wise woman, and she said to Catherine, "You have suffered much, my poor girl, but at length your luck has turned, and I know by the balancing of the scales through the crown that you will die a Queen."

"So she shall," cried the King, who overheard these words; "she shall die my Queen, for she is more beautiful than all the ladies of the court, and I will marry no one else."

And so it fell out. The King sent back the bride he had

The Silk was Always Heavier.

promised to wed to her own country, and the same day Catherine was Queen at the marriage feast instead, and lived happy and contented to the end of her life.

Never again was Queen Catherine annoyed or persecuted by her Destiny; happy with her King, she did all in her power to make others happy as well. She lived to a very good old age, and never had reason to regret having chosen to overcome all her trials and troubles with the strength of her youth, putting off till her later years the happiness she was so richly entitled to.

Catherine Was Queen Instead.

The Prince Bent Down.

THE · FLOWER · QUEEN'S · DAUGHTER

A young Prince was riding one day through a meadow that stretched for miles in front of him, when he came to a deep open ditch. He was turning aside to avoid it, when he heard the sound of someone crying within it. He dismounted from his horse, and stepped along in the direction the sound came from. To his astonishment he found an old woman, who begged him to help her out of the ditch. The Prince bent down and lifted her out of her living grave, asking her at the same time how she had managed to get there.

"My son," answered the old woman, "I am a very poor woman, and soon after midnight I set out for the neighboring town in order to sell my eggs in the market on the following morning; but I lost my way in the dark, and fell into this deep ditch, where I might have remained forever but for your kindness."

Then the Prince said to her, "You can hardly walk; I will put you on my horse and lead you home. Where do you live?"

"Over there, at the edge of the forest in the little hut you see in the distance," replied the old woman.

The Prince lifted her on to his horse, and soon they reached the hut, where the old woman got down, and turning to the Prince said, "Just wait a moment, and I will give you something." And she disappeared into her hut, but returned very soon and said, "You are a mighty Prince, but at the same time you have a kind heart, which deserves to be rewarded. Would you like to have the most beautiful woman in the world for your wife?"

"Most certainly I would," replied the Prince.

So the old woman continued, "The most beautiful woman in the whole world is the daughter of the Queen of the Flowers, who has been captured by a dragon. If you wish to marry her, you must first set her free, and this I will help you to do. I will give you this little bell: if you ring it once, the King of the Eagles will appear; if you ring it twice, the King of the Foxes will come to you; and if you ring it three times, you will see the King of the Fishes by your side. These will help you if you are in any difficulty. Now farewell, and heaven prosper your undertaking." She handed him the little bell, and hut and all disappeared, as though the earth had swallowed them up.

Then it dawned on the Prince that he had been speaking to a good fairy, and putting the little bell carefully in his pocket, he rode home and told his father that he meant to set free the daughter of the Flower Queen, and intended setting out on the following day into the wide world in search of her.

"You are a Mighty Prince."

The Flower Queen's Daughter

So the next morning the Prince mounted his fine horse and left his home. He had roamed round the world for a whole year, and his horse had died of exhaustion, while he himself had suffered much from want and misery, but still he had come on no trace of her he was in search of. At last one day he came to a hut, in front of which sat a very old man. The Prince asked him, "Do you not know where the Dragon lives who keeps the daughter of the Flower Queen prisoner?"

"No, I do not," answered the old man. "But if you go straight along this road for a year, you will reach a hut where my father lives, and possibly he may be able to tell you."

The Prince thanked him for his information, and continued his journey for a whole year along the same road, and at the end of it came to the little hut, where he found a very, very old man. He asked him the same question, and the old man answered, "No, I do not know where the Dragon lives. But go straight along this road for another year, and you will come to a hut in which my father lives. I know he can tell you."

And so the Prince wandered on for another year, always on the same road, and at last reached the hut where he found the third old man.

He put the same question to him as he had put to his son and grandson; but this time the old man answered, "The Dragon lives up there on the mountain, and he has just begun his year of sleep. For one whole year he is always awake, and the next he sleeps. But

He Came to a Hut.

if you wish to see the Flower Queen's daughter go up the second mountain: the Dragon's old mother lives there, and she has a ball every night, to which the Flower Queen's daughter goes regularly."

So the Prince went up the second mountain, where he found a castle all made of gold with diamond windows. He opened the big gate leading into the courtyard, and was just going to walk in, when seven dragons rushed on him and asked him what he wanted!

The Prince replied, "I have heard so much of the beauty and kindness of the Dragon's Mother, and would like to enter her service."

This flattering speech pleased the dragons, and the eldest of them said, "Well, you may come with me, and I will take you to the Mother Dragon."

They entered the castle and walked through twelve splendid halls, all made of gold and diamonds. In the twelfth room they found the Mother Dragon seated on a diamond throne. She was the ugliest woman under the sun, and, added to it all, she had three heads.

Her appearance was a great shock to the Prince, and so was her voice, which was like the croaking of many ravens. She asked him, "Why have you come here?"

The Prince answered at once, "I have heard so much of your beauty and kindness, that I would very much like to enter your service."

"Very well," said the Mother Dragon; "but if you wish to

Seven Dragons Rushed on Him!

enter my service, you must first lead my mare out to the meadow and look after her for three days; but if you don't bring her home safely every evening, we will eat you up."

The Prince undertook the task and led the mare out to the meadow. But no sooner had they reached the grass than she vanished. The Prince sought for her in vain, and at last in despair sat down on a big stone and contemplated his sad fate. As he sat thus lost in thought, he noticed an eagle flying over his head. Then he suddenly bethought him of his little bell, and taking it out of his pocket he rang it once. In a moment he heard a rustling sound in the air beside him, and the King of the Eagles sank at his feet.

"I know what you want of me," the bird said. "You are looking for the Mother Dragon's mare who is galloping about among the clouds. I will summon all the eagles of the air together, and order them to catch the mare and bring her to you." And with these words the King of the Eagles flew away.

Towards evening the Prince heard a mighty rushing sound in the air, and when he looked up he saw thousands of eagles driving the mare before them. They sank at his feet on to the ground and gave the mare over to him.

Then the Prince rode home to the old Mother Dragon, who was full of wonder when she saw him, and said, "You have succeeded today in looking after my mare, and as a reward you shall come to my ball tonight." She gave him at the same time a cloak made of copper, and led him to a big room where several young

The Prince Undertook the Task.

he-dragons and she-dragons were dancing together.

Here, too, was the Flower Queen's beautiful daughter. Her dress was woven out of the most lovely flowers in the world, and her complexion was like lilies and roses. As the Prince was dancing with her he managed to whisper in her ear, "I have come to set you free!"

Then the beautiful girl said to him, "If you succeed in bringing the mare back safely the third day, ask the Mother Dragon to give you a foal of the mare as a reward."

The ball came to an end at midnight, and early next morning the Prince again led the Mother Dragon's mare out into the meadow. But again she vanished before his eyes. Then he took out his little bell and rang it twice.

In a moment the King of the Foxes stood before him and said, "I know already what you want, and will summon all the foxes of the world together to find the mare who has hidden herself in a hill."

With these words the King of the Foxes disappeared, and in the evening many thousand foxes brought the mare to the Prince.

Then he rode home to the Mother Dragon, from whom he received this time a cloak made of silver, and again she led him to the ballroom.

The Flower Queen's daughter was delighted to see him safe and sound, and when they were dancing together she whispered in his ear, "If you succeed again tomorrow, wait for me with the foal

"I Have Come to Set You Free!"

in the meadow. After the ball we will fly away together."

On the third day the Prince led the mare to the meadow again; but once more she vanished before his eyes. Then the Prince took out his little bell and rang it three times.

In a moment the King of the Fishes appeared, and said to him, "I know quite well what you want me to do, and I will summon all the fishes of the sea together, and tell them to bring you back the mare, who is hiding herself in a river."

Towards evening the mare was returned to him, and when he led her home to the Mother Dragon, she said to him,

"You are a brave youth, and I will make you my body servant. But what shall I give you as a reward to begin with?"

The Prince begged for a foal of the mare, which the Mother Dragon at once gave him, and over and above, a cloak made of gold, for she had fallen in love with him because he had praised her beauty.

In the evening he appeared at the ball in his golden cloak; but before the entertainment was over he slipped away, and went straight to the stables, where he mounted his foal and rode out into the meadow to wait for the Flower Queen's daughter. Towards midnight the beautiful girl appeared, and placing her in front of him on his horse, they flew like the wind till they reached the Flower Queen's dwelling.

But the dragons had noticed their flight, and woke their brother out of his year's sleep. He flew into a terrible rage when he

The King of the Fishes Appeared.

heard what had happened, and determined to lay siege to the Flower Queen's palace; but the Queen caused a forest of flowers as high as the sky to grow up round her dwelling, through which no one could force a way.

When the Flower Queen heard that her daughter wanted to marry the Prince, she said to him, "I will give my consent to your marriage gladly, but my daughter can only stay with you in summer. In winter, when everything is dead and the ground covered with snow, she must come and live with me in my palace underground."

The Prince consented to this, and led his beautiful bride home, where the wedding was held with great pomp and magnificence. The young couple lived happily together till winter came, when the Flower Queen's daughter departed and went home to her mother.

In summer she returned to her husband, and their life of joy and happiness began again, and lasted till the approach of winter, when the Flower Queen's daughter went back again to her mother. This coming and going continued all her life long, and in spite of it they always lived happily together.

A Forest of Flowers as High as the Sky

"Will You Sell Me Your Horse?"

THE · ENCHANTED · DEER

A young man named Ian was walking one day, leading a cart-horse by the bridle. He was thinking of his mother and how poor they were since his father, who was a fisherman, had been drowned at sea, and wondering what he should do to earn a living for both of them. Suddenly a hand was laid on his shoulder, and a voice said to him:

"Will you sell me your horse, son of the fisherman?" Looking up he beheld a man standing in the road with a gun in his hand, a falcon on his shoulder, and a dog by his side.

"What will you give me for my horse?" asked Ian. "Will you give me your gun, and your dog, and your falcon?"

"I will give them," answered the man, and he took the horse, and the youth took the gun and the dog and the falcon, and went home with them. But when his mother heard what he had done she was very angry, and beat him with a stick which she had in her hand.

"That will teach you to sell my property," said she, when her arm was quite tired, but Ian her son answered her nothing, and went off to his bed, for he was very sore.

That night he rose softly, and left the house carrying the gun with him. "I will not stay here to be beaten," thought he, and he walked and walked and walked, till it was day again and he was hungry and looked about him to see if he could get anything to eat.

Not very far off was a farmhouse, so he went there, and knocked at the door, and the farmer and his wife begged him to come in, and share their breakfast.

"Ah, you have a gun," said the farmer as the young man placed it in a corner. "That is well, for a deer comes every evening to eat my corn, and I cannot catch it. It is fortune that has sent you to me."

"I will gladly remain and shoot the deer for you," replied the youth, and that night he hid himself and watched till the deer came to the cornfield; then he lifted his gun to his shoulder and was just going to pull the trigger, when, behold! Instead of a deer, a woman with long black hair was standing there.

At this sight his gun almost dropped from his hand in surprise, but as he looked, there was the deer eating the corn again. And thrice this happened, till the deer ran away over the moor, and Ian after her.

On they went, on and on and on, till they reached a cottage which was thatched with heather. With a bound the deer sprang

"I Will Not Stay Here."

on the roof, and lay down where none could see her, but as she did so she called out. "Go in, fisher's son, and eat and drink while you may."

So he entered and found food and wine on the table, but no man, for the house belonged to some robbers, who were still away at their wicked business.

After Ian, the fisher's son, had eaten all he wanted, he hid himself behind a great cask, and very soon he heard a noise, as of men coming through the heather, and the small twigs snapping under their feet. From his dark corner he could see into the room, and he counted four and twenty of them, all big, cross-looking men.

"Some one has been eating our dinner," cried they, "and there was hardly enough for ourselves."

"It is the man who is living under the cask," answered the leader. "Go and kill him, and then come and eat your food and sleep, for we must be off betimes in the morning."

So four of them killed the fisher's son and left him, and then went to bed.

By sunrise they were all out of the house, for they had far to go. And when they had disappeared the deer came off the roof to where the dead man lay, and she shook her head over him, and wax fell from her ear, and he jumped up as well as ever.

"Trust me and eat as you did before, and no harm shall happen to you," said she. So Ian ate and drank, and fell sound asleep under the cask. In the evening the robbers arrived very tired, and

"Eat and Drink While You May."

crosser than they had been yesterday, for their luck had turned, and they had brought back scarcely anything.

"Someone has eaten our dinner again," cried they.

"It is the man under the barrel," answered the captain. "Let four of you go and kill him, but first slay the other four who pretended to kill him last night and didn't, because he is still alive."

Then Ian was killed a second time, and after the rest of the robbers had eaten, they lay down and slept till morning.

No sooner were their faces touched with the sun's rays than they were up and off. Then the deer entered and dropped the healing wax on the dead man, and he was as well as ever. By this time he did not mind what befell him, so sure was he that the deer would take care of him, and in the evening that which had happened before happened again — the four robbers were put to death and the fisher's son also.

Because there was no food left for them to eat, the other robbers were nearly mad with rage, and began to quarrel. From quarrelling they went on to fighting, and fought so hard that by and by they were all stretched dead on the floor.

Then the deer entered, and restored the fisher's son to life, and bidding him follow her, she ran on to a little white cottage where dwelt an old woman and her son, who was thin and dark.

"Here I must leave you," said the deer, "but tomorrow meet me at midday in the church that is yonder." And jumping across the stream, she vanished into a wood.

"Someone Has Eaten Our Dinner Again."

The next day Ian set out for the church, but the old woman of the cottage had gone before him, and had stuck an enchanted stick called "the spike of hurt" in a crack of the door, so that he brushed against it as he stepped across the threshold.

Suddenly he felt so sleepy that he could not stand up, and throwing himself on the ground he sank into a deep slumber, not knowing that the dark lad was watching him.

Nothing could waken him, not even the sound of sweetest music, nor the touch of a lady who bent over him. A sad look came on her face, as she saw it was no use, and at last she gave it up and lifting his arm, wrote her name across his side — "the daughter of the King of the town under the waves."

"I will come tomorrow," she whispered, though he could not hear her, and she went sorrowfully away.

Then he awoke, and when the dark lad told him what had befallen him, he was very grieved. But the dark lad did not tell him of the name that was written underneath his arm.

On the following morning the fisher's son again went to the church, determined that he would not go to sleep, whatever happened. But in his hurry to enter he touched with his hand the spike of hurt, and sank down where he stood, wrapped in slumber.

A second time the air was filled with music, and the lady came in, stepping softly, but though she laid his head on her knee, and combed his hair with a golden comb, his eyes opened not. Then she burst into tears, and placing a beautifully wrought box in

He Sank Into a Deep Slumber.

his pocket she went her way.

The next day the same thing befell the fisher's son, and this time the lady wept more bitterly than before, for she said it was the last chance, and she would never be allowed to come any more, for home she must go.

As soon as the lady had departed the fisher's son awoke, and the dark lad told him of her visit, and how he would never see her as long as he lived. At this the fisher's son felt the cold creeping up to his heart, yet he knew the fault had not been his that sleep had overtaken him.

"I will search the whole world through till I find her," cried Ian, and the dark lad laughed as he heard him. But the fisher's son took no heed, and off he went, following the sun day after day, till his shoes were in holes and his feet were sore from the journey.

Nought did he see but the birds that made their nests in the trees, not so much as a goat or a rabbit. On and on and on he went, till suddenly he came upon a little house, with a woman standing outside it.

"All hail, fisher's son!" said she. "I know what you are seeking; enter in and rest and eat, and tomorrow I will give you what help I can, and send you on your way."

Gladly did Ian the fisher's son accept her offer, and all that day he rested, and the woman gave him ointment to put on his feet, which healed his sores. At daybreak he got up, ready to be gone, and the woman bade him farewell, saying:

The Lady Wept More Bitterly than Before.

"I have a sister who dwells on the road which you must travel. It is a long road, and it would take you a year and a day to reach it, but put on these old brown shoes with holes all over them, and you will be there before you know it. Then shake them off, and turn their toes to the known, and their heels to the unknown, and they will come home of themselves."

The fisher's son did as the woman told him, and everything happened just as she had said. But at parting the second sister said to him, as she gave him another pair of shoes:

"Go to my third sister, for she has a son who is keeper of the birds of the air, and sends them to sleep when night comes. He is very wise, and perhaps he can help you."

Then the young man thanked her, and went to the third sister.

The third sister was very kind, but had no counsel to give him, so he ate and drank and waited till her son came home, after he had sent all the birds to sleep. He thought a long while after his mother had told him the young man's story, and at last he said that he was hungry, and the cow must be killed, as he wanted some supper. So the cow was killed and the meat cooked, and a bag made of its red skin.

"Now get into the bag," bade the son, and Ian got in and took his gun with him, but the dog and the falcon he left outside. The keeper of the birds drew the string at the top of the bag, and left it to finish his supper, when in flew an eagle through the open

"Toes to the Known, Heels to the Unknown"

door, and picked the bag up in her claws and carried it through the air to an island.

There was nothing to eat on the island, and the fisher's son thought he would die for lack of food, when he remembered the box that the lady had put in his pocket. He opened the lid, and three tiny little birds flew out, and flapping their wings they asked,

"Good master, is there anything we can do for thee?"

"Bear me to the kingdom of the King under the waves," he answered, and one little bird flew on to his head, and the others perched on each of his shoulders, and he shut his eyes, and in a moment there he was in the country under the sea.

Then the birds flew away, and the young man looked about him, his heart beating fast at the thought that here dwelt the lady whom he had sought all the world over.

He walked on through the streets, and presently he reached the house of a weaver who was standing at his door, resting from his work.

"You are a stranger here, that is plain," said the weaver, "but come in, and I will give you food and drink." And the young man was glad, for he knew not where to go, and they sat and talked till it grew late.

"Stay with me, I pray, for I love company and am lonely," observed the weaver at last, and he pointed to a bed in a corner, where the fisher's son threw himself and slept till dawn when he was awakened by his host.

Three Tiny Birds Flew Out.

"There is to be a horse race in the town today," remarked the weaver, "and the winner is to have the King's daughter to wife." The young man trembled with excitement at the news, and his voice shook as he answered:

"That will be a prize indeed; I should like to see the race."

"Oh, that is quite easy — anyone can go," replied the weaver. "I could take you myself, but I have promised to weave this cloth for the King."

"That is a pity," returned the young man politely, but in his heart he rejoiced, for he wished to be alone.

Leaving the house, he entered a grove of trees which stood behind, and took the box from his pocket. He raised the lid, and out flew the three little birds.

"Good master, what shall we do for thee?" asked they, and he answered, "Bring me the finest horse that ever was seen, and the grandest dress, and glass shoes."

"They are here, master," said the birds, and so they were, and never had the young man seen anything so splendid.

Mounting the horse he rode into the ground where the horses were assembling for the great race, and took his place among them. Many good beasts were there which had won many races, but the horse of the fisher's son left them all behind, and he was first at the winning post.

The King's daughter waited for him in vain to claim his prize, for he went back to the wood, and got off his horse, and put on his

"The Winner is to Have the King's Daughter to Wife."

old clothes, and bade the box place some gold in his pockets.

After that he went back to the weaver's house, and told him that the gold had been given him by the man who had won the race, and that the weaver might have it for his kindness to him.

Now as nobody had appeared to demand the hand of the Princess, the King ordered another race to be run, and the fisher's son rode into the field still more splendidly dressed than he was before, and easily distanced everybody else. But again he left the prize unclaimed, and so it happened on the third day, when it seemed as if all the people in the kingdom were gathered to see the race, for they were filled with curiosity to know who the winner could be.

"If he will not come of his own free will, he must be brought," said the King, and messengers who had seen the face of the victor were sent to seek him in every street of the town. This took many days, and when at last they found the young man in the weaver's cottage, he was so dirty and had such a strange appearance, that they declared he could not be the winner they had been searching for, but a wicked robber who had murdered ever so many people, but had always managed to escape.

"Yes, it must be the robber," said the King, when the fisher's son was led into his presence. "Build a gallows at once and hang him in the sight of all my subjects, that they may behold him suffer the punishment of his crimes."

So the gallows were built upon a high platform, and the

Another Race to be Run

fisher's son mounted the steps up to it, and turned at the top to make the speech that was expected from every doomed man, innocent or guilty. As he spoke, he happened to raise his arm, and the King's daughter, who was there at her father's side, saw the name which she had written under it. With a shriek she sprang from her seat, and the eyes of all the spectators were turned towards her.

"Stop! Stop!" she cried, hardly knowing what she said. "If that man is hanged there is not a soul in the kingdom but shall die also." And running up to where the fisher's son was standing, she took him by the hand, saying:

"Father, this is no robber or murderer, but the victor in the three races, and he loosed the spells that were laid upon me."

Then, without waiting for a reply, she conducted him into the palace, and he bathed in a marble bath, and all the dirt that the fairies had put upon him disappeared like magic, and when he had dressed himself in the fine garments the Princess had sent to him, he looked a match for any King's daughter. He went down into the great hall where she was awaiting him, and they had much to tell each other but little time to tell it in, for the King her father, and the Princes who were visiting him, and all the people of the kingdom were still in their places expecting her return.

"How did you find me out?" she whispered as they went down the passage

"The birds in the box told me," answered he, but he could say no more, as they stepped out into the open space that was

She Sprang From Her Seat.

crowded with people. There the Princess stopped.

"O Kings!" she said, turning towards them, "If one of you were killed today, the rest would fly; but this man put his trust in me, and had his head cut off three times. Because he has done this, I will marry him rather than one of you, who have come hither to wed me, for many Kings here sought to free me from the spells, but none could do it save Ian the fisher's son."

With that she took his arm, and led him to where her father, the King, sat on his golden throne. The King blessed them both, blessed their marriage which took place in the most splendid fashion the very next day, and the fisher's son, now Prince Ian, and his lovely wife blessed the King with many grandchildren in the years that followed.

"None Could Do It Save Ian."

A Ship to Float on Both Land and Sea

HOW · THE · HERMIT · HELPED · WIN · THE · PRINCESS

Long ago there lived a very rich man who had three sons. When he felt himself to be dying he divided his property amongst them, making them share alike, both in money and lands. Soon after he died the King set forth a proclamation through the whole country that whoever could build a ship that should float both on land and sea should have his daughter to wife.

The eldest brother, when he heard it, said to the others, "I think I will spend some of my money in trying to build that ship, as I should like to have the King for my father-in-law."

So he called together all the shipbuilders in the land, and gave them orders to begin the ship without delay. Trees were cut down, and great preparations made, and in a few days everybody knew what it was all for; and there was a crowd of old people pressing round the gates of the yard, where the young man spent the most of his day.

"Ah, master, give us work," they said, "so that we may earn our bread."

But he only gave them hard words, and spoke roughly to them. "You are old, and have lost your strength; of what use are you?" And he drove them away. Then came some boys and prayed him, "Master, give us work," but he answered them, "Of what use can you be, weaklings as you are! Get you gone!" And if any presented themselves that were not skilled workmen he would have none of them.

At last there knocked at the gate a little old man with a long white beard who said, "Will you give me work, so that I may earn my bread?" But he was only driven away like the rest.

The ship took a long while to build, and cost a great deal of money, and when it was launched a sudden squall rose, and it fell to pieces, and with it all the young man's hopes of winning the Princess. By this time he had not a penny left, so he went back to his two brothers and told his tale.

And the second brother said to himself as he listened, "Certainly he has managed very badly, but I should like to see if I can't do better, and win the Princess for my own self." So he called together all the shipbuilders throughout the country, and gave them orders to build a ship which should float on the land as well as on the sea.

But his heart was no softer than his brother's, and every man who was not a skilled workman was chased away with hard words.

Driven Away, Like the Rest

Last came the white-bearded man, but he fared no better than the rest.

When the ship was finished the launch took place, and everything seemed going smoothly when a gale sprang up, and the vessel was dashed to pieces on the rocks. The young man had spent his whole fortune on it, and now it was all swallowed up, he was forced to beg shelter from his youngest brother.

When he told his story the youngest said to himself, "I am not rich enough to support us all three. I had better take my turn, and if I manage to win the Princess there will be her fortune as well as my own for us to live on."

So he called together all the shipbuilders in the kingdom, and gave orders that a new ship should be built. Then all the old people came and asked for work, and he answered cheerfully, "Oh, yes, there is plenty for everybody;" and when the boys begged to be allowed to help he found something that they could do.

And when the old man with the long white beard stood before him, praying that he might earn his bread, he replied, "Oh, father, I could not suffer you to work, but you shall be overseer, and look after the rest."

Now the old man was a holy hermit, and when he saw how kind-hearted the youth was, he determined to do all he could for him to gain the wish of his heart.

By and by, when the ship was finished, the hermit said to his young friend, "Now you can go and claim the King's daughter, for

"I Am Not Rich Enough."

the ship will float both by land and sea."

"Oh, good father," cried the young man, "you will not forsake me? Stay with me, I pray you, and lead me to the King!"

"If you wish it, I will," said the hermit, "on condition that you will give me half of anything you get."

"Oh, if that is all," answered he, "it is easily promised!" And they set out together on the ship.

After they had gone some distance they saw a man standing in a thick fog, which he was trying to put into a sack.

"Oh, good father," exclaimed the youth, "what can he be doing?"

"Ask him," said the old man.

"What are you doing, my fine fellow?"

"I am putting the fog into my sack. That is my business."

"Ask him if he will come with us," whispered the hermit.

And the man answered: "If you will give me enough to eat and drink I will gladly stay with you."

So they took him on their ship, and the youth said, as they started off again, "Good father, before we were two, and now we are three!"

After they had travelled a little further they met a man who had torn up half the forest, and was carrying all the trees on his shoulders.

"Good father," exclaimed the youth, "only look! What can he have done that for?"

"I Am Putting the Fog Into My Sack."

"Ask him why he has torn up all those trees."

And the man replied, "Why, I've merely been gathering a handful of brushwood."

"Beg him to come with us," whispered the hermit.

And the strong man answered, "Willingly, as long as you give me enough to eat and drink." And he came on the ship.

And the youth said to the hermit, "Good father, before we were three, and now we are four."

The ship travelled on again, and some miles further on they saw a man drinking out of a stream till he had nearly drunk it dry.

"Good father," said the youth, "just look at that man! Did you ever see anybody drink like that?"

"Ask him why he does it," answered the hermit.

"Why, there is nothing very odd in taking a mouthful of water!" replied the man, standing up.

"Beg him to come with us." And the youth did so.

"With pleasure, as long as you give me enough to eat and drink."

And the youth whispered to the hermit, "Good father, before we were four, and now we are five."

A little way along they noticed another man in the middle of a stream, who was shooting into the water.

"Good father," said the youth, "what can he be shooting at?"

"Ask him," answered the hermit.

"Hush, hush!" cried the man. "Now you have frightened it

"A Handful of Brushwood."

away. In the Underworld sits a quail on a tree, and I wanted to shoot it. That is my business. I hit everything I aim at."

"Ask him if he will come with us."

And the man replied, "With all my heart, as long as I get enough to eat and drink."

So they took him into the ship, and the young man whispered, "Good father, before we were five, and now we are six."

Off they went again, and before they had gone far they met a man striding towards them whose steps were so long that while one foot was on the north of the island the other was right down in the south.

"Good father, look at him! What long steps he takes!"

"Ask him why he does it," replied the hermit.

"Oh, I am only going out for a little walk," answered he.

"Ask him if he will come with us."

"Gladly, if you will give me as much as I want to eat and drink," said he, climbing up into the ship.

And the young man whispered, "Good father, before we were six, and now we are seven." But the hermit knew what he was doing, and why he gathered these strange people into the ship.

After many days, at last they reached the town where lived the King and his daughter. They stopped the vessel right in front of the palace, and the young man went in and bowed low before the king.

"O Majesty, I have done your bidding, and now is the ship

"I Hit Everything I Aim At."

built that can travel over land and sea. Give me my regard, and let me have your daughter to wife."

But the King said to himself, "What! Am I to wed my daughter to a man of whom I know nothing? Not even whether he be rich or poor — a knight or a beggar."

And aloud he spoke: "It is not enough that you have managed to build the ship. You must find a runner who shall take this letter to the ruler of the Underworld, and bring me the answer back in an hour."

"That is not in the bond," answered the young man.

"Well, do as you like," replied the King, "only you will not get my daughter."

The young man went out, sorely troubled, to tell his old friend what had happened.

"Silly boy!" cried the hermit. "Accept his terms at once. And send off the long-legged man with the letter. He will take it in no time at all."

So the youth's heart leapt for joy, and he returned to the King. "Majesty, I accept your terms. Here is the messenger who will do what you wish."

The King had no choice but to give the man the letter, and he strode off, making short work of the distance that lay between the palace and the Underworld.

He soon found the ruler, who looked at the letter, and said to him, "Wait a little while I write the answer;" but the man was so

"It Is Not Enough."

tired with his quick walk that he went sound asleep, and forgot all about his errand.

All this time the youth was anxiously counting the minutes till he could get back, and stood with his eyes fixed on the road down which his messenger must come.

"What can be keeping him?" he said to the hermit when the hour was nearly up.

Then the hermit sent for the man who could hit every thing he aimed at, and said to him, "Just see why the messenger stays so long."

"Oh, he is sound asleep in the palace of the Underworld. However, I can soon wake him." Then he drew his bow, and shot an arrow straight into the man's knee. The messenger awoke with a start, and when he saw that the hour had almost run out he snatched up the answer and rushed back with such speed that the clock had not yet struck when he entered the palace.

Now the young man thought he was sure of his bride, but the King said, "Still you have not done enough. Before I give you my daughter you must find a man who can drink half the contents of my cellar in one day."

"That is not in the bond," complained the poor youth.

"Well, do as you like, only you will not get my daughter."

The young man went sadly out, and asked the hermit what he was to do.

"Silly boy!" said he. "Why, tell the man to do it who drinks

"I Can Soon Wake Him."

up everything."

So they sent for the man and said, "Do you think you are able to drink half the royal cellar in one day?"

"Dear me, yes, and as much more as you want," answered he. "I am never satisfied."

The King was not pleased at the young man agreeing so readily, but he had no choice, and ordered the servant to be taken downstairs. Oh, how he enjoyed himself! All day long he drank, and drank, and drank, till, instead of half the cellar, he had drunk the whole, and there was not a cask but what stood empty.

When the King saw this he said to the youth, "You have conquered, and I can no longer withhold my daughter. But, as her dowry, I shall only give so much as one man can carry away."

"But," answered he, "let a man be ever so strong, he cannot carry more than a hundredweight, and what is that for a King's daughter?"

"Well, do as you like; I have said my say. It is your affair — not mine."

The young man was puzzled, and did not know what to reply, for, though he would gladly have married the Princess without a sixpence, he had spent all his money in building the ship, and knew he could not give her all she wanted.

So he went to the hermit and said to him, "The King will only give for her dowry as much as a man can carry. I have no money of my own left, and my brothers have none either."

"Drink Half the Royal Cellar in One Day."

"Silly boy! Why, you have only got to fetch the man who carried half the forest on his shoulders."

And the youth was glad, and called the strong man, and told him what he must do. "Take everything you can, till you are bent double. Never mind if you leave the palace bare."

The strong man promised, and nobly kept his word. He piled all he could see on his back — chairs, tables, wardrobes, chests of gold and silver — till there was nothing left to pile. At last he took the King's crown, and put it on the top. He carried his burden to the ship and stowed his treasures away, and the youth followed, leading the King's daughter.

But the King was left raging in his empty palace, and he called together his army, and got ready his ships of war, in order that he might go after the vessel and bring back what had been taken away.

And the King's ships sailed very fast, and soon caught up with the little vessel, and the sailors all shouted for joy. Then the hermit looked out and saw how near they were, and he said to the youth, "Do you see that?"

The youth shrieked and cried, "Ah, good father, it is a fleet of ships, and they are chasing us, and in a few moments they will be upon us!"

But the hermit bade him call the man who had the fog in his sack, and the sack was opened and the fog flew out, and hung right round the King's ships, so that they could see nothing. So they sailed back to the palace, and told the King what strange things

He Piled All on His Back.

had happened. Meanwhile the young man's vessel reached home in safety.

"Well, here you are once more," said the hermit; "and now you can fulfill the promise you made me to give me the half of all you had."

"That will I do with all my heart," answered the youth, and began to divide all his treasures, putting part on one side for himself and setting aside the other for his friend. "Good father, it is finished," said he at length; "there is nothing more left to divide."

"Nothing more left!" cried the hermit. "Why, you have forgotten the best thing of all!"

"What can that be?" asked he. "We have divided everything."

"And the King's daughter?" said the hermit.

Then the young man's heart stood still, for he loved her dearly. But he answered, "It is well; I have sworn, and I will keep my word," and drew his sword to cut her in pieces.

When the hermit saw that he held his honor dearer than his wife, he lifted his hand and cried "Hold! She is yours, and all the treasures too. I gave you my help because you had pity on those that were in need. And when you are in need yourself, call upon me, and I will come to you."

As he spoke, he softly touched their heads and vanished.

The next day the wedding took place, and the two brothers came to the house, and they all lived happily together, but they never forgot the holy man who had been such a good friend.

"And the King's Daughter?"

Martin, Michael, and Jack

THE · THREE · TREASURES · OF · THE · GIANTS

L ong, long ago, there lived an old man and his wife who had three sons; the eldest was called Martin, the second Michael, while the third was named Jack.

One evening they were all seated round the table, eating their supper of bread and milk.

"Martin," said the old man suddenly, "I feel that I cannot live much longer. You, as the eldest, will inherit this hut, but, if you value my blessing, be good to your mother and brothers."

"Certainly, father; how can you suppose I should do them wrong?" replied Martin indignantly, helping himself to all the best bits in the dish as he spoke. The old man saw nothing, but Michael looked on in surprise, and Jack was so astonished that he quite forgot to eat his own supper.

A little while after, the father fell ill, and sent for his sons, who were out hunting, to bid him farewell. After giving good advice to the two eldest, he turned to Jack.

"My boy," he said, "you have not got quite as much sense as other people, but if Heaven has deprived you of some of your wits, it has given you a kind heart. Always listen to what it says, and take heed to the words of your mother and brothers, as well as you are able!" So saying the old man sank back on his pillows and died.

The cries of grief uttered by Martin and Michael sounded through the house, but Jack remained by the bedside of his father, still and silent, as if he were dead also. At length he got up, and going into the garden, hid himself in some trees, and wept like a child, while his two brothers made ready for the funeral.

No sooner was the old man buried than Martin and Michael agreed that they would go into the world together to seek their fortunes, while Jack stayed at home with their mother. Jack would have liked nothing better than to sit and dream by the fire, but the mother, who was very old herself, declared that there was no work for him to do, and that he must seek it with his brothers.

So, one fine morning, all three set out; Martin and Michael carried two great bags full of food, but Jack carried nothing. This made his brothers very angry, for the day was hot and the bags were heavy, and about noon they sat down under a tree and began to eat.

Jack was as hungry as they were, but he knew that it was no use asking for anything; and he threw himself under another tree, and wept bitterly.

One Fine Morning All Three Set Out.

"Another time perhaps you won't be so lazy, and will bring food for yourself," said Martin, but to his surprise Jack answered:

"You are a nice pair! You talk of seeking your fortunes so as not to be a burden on our mother, and you begin by carrying off all the food she has in the house!"

This reply was so unexpected that for some moments neither of the brothers made any answer. Then they offered their brother some of their food, and when he had finished eating they went their way once more.

Towards evening they reached a small hut, and knocking at the door, asked if they might spend the night there. The man, who was a wood-cutter, invited them in, and begged them to sit down to supper.

Martin thanked him, but being very proud, explained that it was only shelter they wanted, as they had plenty of food with them; he and Michael at once opened their bags and began to eat, while Jack hid himself in a corner.

The wife, on seeing this, took pity on him, and called him to come and share their supper, which he gladly did, and very good he found it. At this, Martin regretted deeply that he had been so foolish as to refuse, for his bits of bread and cheese seemed very hard when he smelt the savory soup his brother was enjoying.

"He shan't have such a chance again," thought he; and the next morning he insisted on plunging into a thick forest where they were likely to meet nobody.

"You are a Nice Pair!"

For a long time they wandered hither and thither, for they had no path to guide them; but at last they came upon a wide clearing, in the midst of which stood a castle. Jack shouted with delight, but Martin, who was in a bad temper, said sharply:

"We must have taken a wrong turn! Let us go back."

"Idiot!" replied Michael, who was hungry, too, and like many people when they are hungry, very cross also. "We set out to travel through the world, and what does it matter if we go to the right or to the left?" And, without another word, he took the path to the castle, closely followed by Jack, and after a moment by Martin likewise.

The door of the castle stood open, and they entered a great hall, and looked about them. Not a creature was to be seen, and suddenly Martin — he did not know why — felt a little frightened.

He would have left the castle at once, but stopped when Jack boldly walked up to a door in the wall and opened it. He could not for very shame be outdone by his younger brother, and passed behind him into another splendid hall, which was filled from floor to ceiling with great pieces of copper money.

The sight quite dazzled Martin and Michael, who emptied all the provisions that remained out of their bags, and heaped them up instead with handfuls of copper.

Scarcely had they done this when Jack threw open another door, and this time it led to a hall filled with silver. In an instant

The Door of the Castle Stood Open.

his brothers had turned their bags upside down, so that the copper money tumbled out on to the floor, and were shovelling in handfuls of the silver instead.

They had hardly finished, when Jack opened yet a third door, and all three fell back in amazement, for this room was a mass of gold, so bright that their eyes grew sore as they looked at it. However, they soon recovered from their surprise, and quickly emptied their bags of the silver, and filled them with gold instead. When they would hold no more, Martin said:

"We had better hurry off now lest somebody else should come, and we might not know what to do;" and, followed by Michael, he hastily left the castle. Jack lingered behind for a few minutes to put pieces of gold, silver, and copper into his pocket, and to eat the food that his brothers had thrown down in the first room.

Then he went after them, and found them lying down to rest in the midst of a forest. It was near sunset, and Martin began to feel hungry, so, when Jack arrived, he bade him return to the castle and bring the bread and cheese that they had left there.

"It is hardly worth doing that," answered Jack; "for I picked up the pieces and ate them myself."

At this reply both brothers were beside themselves with anger, and fell upon the boy, beating him, and calling him names, till they were quite tired.

"Go where you like," cried Martin with a final kick; "but

This Room was a Mass of Gold.

never come near us again." And poor Jack ran weeping into the woods.

The next morning his brothers went home, and bought a beautiful house, where they lived with their mother like great lords.

Jack remained for some hours in hiding, thankful to be safe from his tormentors; but when no one came to trouble him, and his back did not ache so much, he began to think what he had better do. At length he made up his mind to go to the castle and take away as much money with him as would enable him to live in comfort for the rest of his life.

This being decided, he sprang up, and set out along the path which led to the castle. As before, the door stood open, and he went on till he had reached the hall of gold, and there he took off his jacket and tied the sleeves together so that it might make a kind of bag. He then began to pour in the gold by handfuls, when, all at once, a noise like thunder shook the castle. This was followed by a voice, hoarse as that of a bull, which cried:

"I smell the smell of a man." And two giants entered.

"So, little worm! It is *you*, who steal our treasures!" exclaimed the biggest. "Well, we have got you now, and we will cook you for supper!" But here the other giant drew him aside, and for a moment or two they whispered together. At length the first giant spoke:

"To please my friend I will spare your life on condition that,

He Made Up His Mind.

for the future, you shall guard our treasures. If you are hungry take this little table and rap on it, saying as you do so: 'The dinner of an Emperor!' and you will get as much food as you want."

With a light heart Jack promised all that was asked of him, and for some days enjoyed himself mightily. He had everything he could wish for, and did nothing from morning till night; but by-and-by he began to get very tired of it all.

"Let the giants guard their treasures themselves," he said to himself at last; "I am going away. But I will leave all the gold and silver behind me, and will take nought but you, my good little table."

So, tucking the table under his arm, he started off for the forest, but he did not linger there long, and soon found himself in the fields on the other side. There he saw an old man, who begged Jack to give him something to eat.

"You could not have asked a better person," answered Jack cheerfully. And signing to him to sit down with him under a tree, he set the table in front of them, and struck it three times, crying:

"The dinner of an Emperor!" He had hardly uttered the words when fish and meat of all kinds appeared on it!

"That is a clever trick of yours," said the old man, when he had eaten as much as he wanted. "Give it to me in exchange for a treasure I have which is still better. Do you see this cornet? Well, you have only to tell it that you wish for an army, and you will have as many soldiers as you require."

"The Dinner of an Emperor!"

Now, since he had been left to himself, Jack had grown ambitious, so, after a moment's hesitation, he took the cornet and gave the table in exchange. The old man bade him farewell, and set off down one path, while Jack chose another, and for a long time he was quite pleased with his new possession.

Then, as he felt hungry, he wished for his table back again, as no house was in sight, and he wanted some supper badly. All at once he remembered his cornet, and a wicked thought entered his mind.

"Two hundred hussars, forward!" cried he. And the neighing of horses and the clanking of swords were heard close at hand. The officer who rode at their head approached Jack, and politely inquired what he wished them to do.

"A mile or two along that road," answered Jack, "you will find an old man carrying a table. Take the table from him and bring it to me."

The officer saluted and went back to his men, who started at a gallop to do Jack's bidding.

In ten minutes they had returned, bearing the table with them.

"That is all, thank you," said Jack; and the soldiers disappeared inside the cornet.

Oh, what a good supper Jack had that night, quite forgetting that he owed it to a mean trick. The next day he breakfasted early, and then walked on towards the nearest town. On

"Two Hundred Hussars, Forward!"

the way thither he met another old man, who begged for something to eat.

"Certainly, you shall have something to eat," replied Jack. And, placing the table on the ground, he cried:

"The dinner of an Emperor!" and all sorts of good dishes appeared. At first the old man ate greedily, and said nothing; but, after his hunger was satisfied, he turned to Jack and said:

"That is a very clever trick of yours. Give the table to me, and you shall have something still better."

"I don't believe that there's anything better," answered Jack.

"Yes, there is. Here is my bag; it will give you as many castles as you can possibly want."

Jack thought for a moment; then he replied: "Very well, I will exchange with you." And passing the table to the old man, he hung the bag over his arm.

Five minutes later he summoned five hundred lancers out of the cornet and bade them go after the old man and fetch back the table.

Now that by his cunning he had obtained possession of the three magic objects, he resolved to return to his native place. Smearing his face with dirt, and tearing his clothes so as to look like a beggar, he stopped the passersby and, on pretense of seeking money or food, he questioned them about the village gossip.

In this manner he learned that his brothers had become great men, much respected in all the country round. When he heard

"My Bag Will Give You Many Castles."

that, he lost no time in going to the door of their fine house and imploring them to give him food and shelter; but the only thing he got was hard words, and a command to beg elsewhere.

At length, however, at their mother's entreaty, he was told that he might pass the night in the stable. Here he waited until everybody in the house was sound asleep, when he drew his bag from under his cloak, and desired that a castle might appear in that place; and the cornet gave him soldiers to guard the castle, while the table furnished him with a good supper.

In the morning, he caused it all to vanish, and when his brothers entered the stable they found him lying on the straw.

Jack remained here for many days, doing nothing, and — as far as anybody knew — eating nothing. This conduct puzzled his brothers greatly, and they put such constant questions to him, that at length he told them the secret of the table, and even gave a dinner to them, which far outdid any they had ever seen or heard of.

But though they had solemnly promised to reveal nothing, somehow or other the tale leaked out, and before long reached the ears of the King himself. That very evening his chamberlain arrived at Jack's dwelling, with a request from the King that he might borrow the table for three days.

"Very well," answered Jack, "you can take it back with you. But tell his majesty that if he does not return it at the end of the three days I will make war upon him."

So the chamberlain carried away the table and took it straight

Passing the Night in the Stable

to the King, telling him at the same time of Jack's threat, at which they both laughed till their sides ached.

Now the King was so delighted with the table, and the dinners it gave him, that when the three days were over he could not make up his mind to part with it. Instead, he sent for his carpenter, and bade him copy it exactly, and when it was done he told his chamberlain to return it to Jack with his best thanks.

It happened to be dinner time, and Jack invited the chamberlain, who knew nothing of the trick, to stay and dine with him. The good man, who had eaten several excellent meals provided by the table in the last three days, accepted the invitation with pleasure, even though he was to dine in a stable, and sat down on the straw beside Jack.

"The dinner of an Emperor!" cried Jack. But not even a morsel of cheese made its appearance.

"The dinner of an Emperor!" shouted Jack in a voice of thunder. Then the truth dawned on him; and, crushing the table between his hands, he turned to the chamberlain, who, bewildered and half-frightened, was wondering how to get away.

"Tell your false King that tomorrow I will destroy his castle as easily as I have broken this table."

The chamberlain hastened back to the palace, and gave the King Jack's message, at which he laughed more than before, and called all his courtiers to hear the story. But they were not quite so merry when they woke next morning and beheld ten thousand

The Chamberlain to Stay and Dine

horsemen, and as many archers, surrounding the palace. The King saw it was useless to hold out, and he took the white flag of truce in one hand, and the real table in the other, and set out to look for Jack.

"I committed a crime," said he; "but I will do my best to make up for it. Here is your table, which I own with shame that I tried to steal, and you shall have besides my daughter as your wife!"

There was no need to delay the marriage when the table was able to furnish the most splendid banquet that ever was seen, and after everyone had eaten and drunk as much as they wanted, Jack took his bag and commanded a castle filled with all sorts of treasures to arise in the park for himself and his bride.

At this proof of his power the King's heart died within him.

"Your magic is greater than mine," he said; "and you are young and strong, while I am old and tired. Take, therefore, the sceptre from my hand, and my crown from my head, and rule my people better than I have done."

So at last Jack's ambition was satisfied. He could not hope to be more than a King, and as long as he had his cornet to provide him with soldiers he was secure against his enemies. He never forgave his brothers for the way they had treated him, though he presented his mother with a beautiful castle, and everything she could possibly wish for.

In the center of his own palace was a treasure chamber, and in this chamber the table, the cornet, and the bag were kept as the

The King Saw It Was Useless.

most prized of all his possessions, and not a week passed without a visit from him to make sure they were safe. He reigned long and well, and died a very old man, beloved by his people.

But his good example was not followed by his sons and his grandsons. They grew so proud that they were ashamed to think that the founder of their line had once been a poor boy; and as they and all the world could not fail to remember it, as long as the table, the cornet, and the bag were shown in the treasure chamber, one King, more foolish than the rest, thrust them into a dark and damp cellar.

For some time the kingdom remained, though it became weaker and weaker every year that passed. Then, one day, a rumor reached the King that a large army was marching against him. Vaguely he recollected some tales he had heard about a magic cornet which could provide as many soldiers as would serve to conquer the earth, and which had been removed by his grandfather to a cellar.

Thither he hastened that he might renew his power once more, and in that black and slimy spot he found the treasures indeed. But the table fell to pieces as he touched it, in the cornet there remained only a few fragments of leathern belts which the rats had gnawed, and in the bag nothing but broken bits of stone.

And the King bowed his head to the doom that awaited him, and in his heart cursed the ruin wrought by the pride and foolishness of himself and his forefathers.

Not a Week Passed Without a Visit

The Rock was Called Ahtola.

THE · SEA · KING'S · GIFT

There was once a fisherman who was called Matte. He lived by the shore of the big sea; where else could he live? He had a wife called Maie; could you find a better name for her? In winter they dwelt in a little cottage by the shore, but in spring they flitted to a red rock out in the sea and stayed there the whole summer until it was autumn. The cottage on the rock was even smaller than the other; it had a wooden bolt instead of an iron lock to the door, a stone hearth, a flagstaff, and a weathercock on the roof.

The rock was called Ahtola, and was not larger than the market-place of a town. Between the crevices there grew a little rowan tree and four alder bushes. Heaven only knows how they ever came there; perhaps they were brought by the winter storms.

Besides that, there flourished some tufts of velvety grass, some scattered reeds, two plants of the yellow herb called tansy, four of a red flower, and a pretty white one; but the treasures of the rock consisted of three roots of garlic, which Maie had put in a cleft.

Rock walls sheltered them on the north side, and the sun

shone on them on the south. This does not seem much, but it sufficed Maie for a herb plot.

All good things go in threes, so Matte and his wife fished for salmon in spring, for herring in summer, and for cod in winter. When on Saturdays the weather was fine and the wind favorable, they sailed to the nearest town, sold their fish, and went to church on Sunday.

But it often happened that for weeks at a time they were quite alone on the rock Ahtola, and had nothing to look at except their little yellow-brown dog, which bore the grand name of Prince, their grass tufts, their bushes and blooms, the sea bays and fish, a stormy sky, and the blue, white-crested waves. For the rock lay far away from the land, and there were no green islets or human habitations for miles round; only here and there appeared a rock of the same red stone as Ahtola, besprinkled day and night with the ocean spray.

Matte and Maie were industrious, hard-working folk, happy and contented in their poor hut, and they thought themselves rich when they were able to salt as many casks of fish as they required for winter and yet have some left over with which to buy tobacco for the old man, and a pound or two of coffee for his wife, with plenty of burned corn and chicory in it.

Besides that, they had bread, butter, fish, a beer cask, and a buttermilk jar; what more did they require? All would have gone well had not Maie been possessed with a secret longing which

Salmon, Herring, and Cod

never let her rest; and this was, how she could manage to become the owner of a cow.

"What would you do with a cow?" asked Matte. "She could not swim so far, and our boat is not large enough to bring her over here; and even if we had her, we have nothing to feed her on."

"We have four alder bushes and sixteen tufts of grass," rejoined Maie.

"Yes, of course," laughed Matte, "and we also have three plants of garlic. Garlic would be fine feeding for her."

"Every cow likes salt herring," rejoined his wife. "Even Prince is fond of fish."

"That may be," said her husband. "Methinks she would soon be a dear cow if we had to feed her on salt herring. All very well for Prince, who fights with the gulls over the last morsel. Put the cow out of your head, mother, we are very well off as we are."

Maie sighed. She knew well that her husband was right, but she could not give up the idea of a cow. The buttermilk no longer tasted as good as usual in the coffee; she thought of sweet cream and fresh butter, and of how there was nothing in the world to be compared with them.

One day as Matte and his wife were cleaning herring on the shore they heard Prince barking, and soon there appeared a gaily painted boat with three young men in it, steering towards the rock. They were students, on a boating excursion, and wanted to get something to eat.

The Idea of a Cow

"Bring us a pudding, good mother," cried they to Maie.

"Ah! If only I had such a thing!" sighed Maie.

"A can of fresh milk, then," said the students; "but it must not be skim."

"Yes, if only I had it!" sighed the old woman, still more deeply.

"What! Haven't you got a cow?"

Maie was silent. This question so struck her to the heart that she could not reply. "We have no cow," Matte answered; "but we have good smoked herring, and can cook them in a couple of hours."

"All right, then, that will do," said the students, as they flung themselves down on the rock, while fifty silvery-white herring were turning on the spit in front of the fire.

"What's the name of this little stone in the middle of the ocean?" asked one of them.

"Ahtola," answered the old man.

"Well, you should want for nothing when you live in the Sea King's dominion."

Matte did not understand. He had never read about and knew nothing of the sea gods of old, but the students proceeded to explain to him.

"Ahti," said they, "is a mighty king who lives in his dominion of Ahtola, and has a rock at the bottom of the sea, and possesses besides a treasury of good things. He rules over all fish and animals

"Bring Us a Pudding!"

of the deep; he has the finest cows and the swiftest horses that ever chewed grass at the bottom of the ocean. He who stands well with Ahti is soon a rich man, but one must beware in dealing with him, for he is very changeful and touchy.

"Even a little stone thrown into the water might offend him, and then as he takes back his gift, he stirs up the sea into a storm and drags the sailors down into the depths. Ahti owns also the fairest maidens, who bear the train of his queen Wellamos, and at the sound of music they comb their long, flowing locks, which glisten in the water."

"Oh!" cried Matte, "Have your worships really seen all that?"

"We have as good as seen it," said the students. "It is all printed in a book, and everything printed is true."

"I'm not so sure of that," said Matte, as he shook his head.

But the herring were now ready, and the students ate enough for six, and gave Prince some cold meat which they happened to have in the boat. Prince sat on his hind legs with delight and mewed like a pussy cat. When all was finished, the students handed Matte a shining silver coin, and allowed him to fill his pipe with a special tobacco.

They then thanked him for his kind hospitality and went on their journey, much regretted by Prince, who sat with a woeful expression and whined on the shore as long as he could see a flip of the boat's white sail in the distance.

Maie had never uttered a word, but thought all the more. She

"He Who Stands Well With Ahti is Soon Rich."

had good ears, and had laid to heart the story about Ahti. "How delightful," thought she to herself, "to possess a fairy cow! How delicious every morning and evening to draw milk from it, and yet have no trouble about the feeding, and to keep a shelf near the window for dishes of milk and puddings! But this will never be my luck."

"What are you thinking of?" asked Matte.

"Nothing," said his wife; but all the time she was pondering over some magic rhymes she had heard in her childhood from an old lame man, which were supposed to bring luck in fishing.

"What if I were to try?" thought she.

Now this was Saturday, and on Saturday evening Matte never set the herring-net, for he did not fish on Sunday. Towards evening, however, his wife said:

"Let us set the herring-net just this once."

"No," said her husband, "it is a Saturday night."

"Last night was so stormy, and we caught so little," urged his wife; "tonight the sea is like a mirror, and with the wind in this direction the herring are drawing towards land."

"But there are streaks in the north-western sky, and Prince was eating grass this evening," said the old man.

"Surely he has not eaten my garlic," exclaimed the old woman.

"No, but there will be rough weather by to-morrow at sunset," rejoined Matte.

He Did Not Fish on Sunday.

"Listen to me," said his wife, "we will set only one net close to the shore, and then we shall be able to finish up our half-filled cask, which will spoil if it stands open so long."

The old man allowed himself to be talked over, and so they rowed out with the net. When they reached the deepest part of the water, she began to hum the words of the magic rhyme, altering the words to suit the longings of her heart:

Oh, Ahti, with the long, long beard,
    Who dwellest in the deep blue sea,
Finest treasures, have I heard,
    And glittering fish belong to thee.
The richest pearls beyond compare
    Are stored up in thy realm below,
And Ocean's cows so sleek and fair
    Feed on the grass in thy green meadow.

King of the waters, far and near,
    I ask not of thy golden store,
I wish not jewels of pearl to wear,
    Nor silver either, ask I for,
But one is odd and even is two,
    So give me a cow, Sea King so bold,
And in return I'll give to you
    A slice of the moon, and the sun's gold.

So They Rowed Out.

"What's that you're humming?" asked the old man.

"Oh, only the words of an old rhyme that keeps running in my head," answered the old woman, and she raised her voice and went on:

> Oh, Ahti, with the long, long beard,
>> Who dwellest in the deep blue sea
> A thousand cows are in thy herd,
>> I pray thee give one unto me.

"That's a stupid sort of song," said Matte. "What else should one beg of the Sea King but fish? But such songs are not for Sunday."

His wife pretended not to hear him, and sang and sang the same tune all the time they were on the water. Matte heard nothing more as he sat and rowed the heavy boat, while thinking of his cracked pipe and the fine tobacco. Then they returned to the island, and soon after went to bed.

But neither Matte nor Maie could sleep a wink; the one thought of how he had profaned Sunday, and the other of Ahti's cow.

About midnight the fisherman sat up, and said to his wife:

"Dost thou hear anything?"

"No," said she.

"I think the twirling of the weathercock on the roof bodes ill," said he; "we shall have a storm."

Maie Raised Her Voice and Went On.

"Oh, it is nothing but your fancy," said his wife.

Matte lay down, but soon rose again.

"The weathercock is squeaking now," said he.

"Just fancy! Go to sleep," said his wife; and the old man tried to.

For the third time he jumped out of bed.

"Ho! How the weathercock is roaring at the pitch of its voice, as if it had a fire inside it! We are going to have a tempest, and must bring in the net."

Both rose. The summer night was as dark as if it had been October, the weathercock creaked, and the storm was raging in every direction. As they went out, the sea lay around them as white as snow, and the spray was dashing right over the fisher-hut.

In all his life Matte had never remembered such a night. To launch the boat and put to sea to rescue the net was a thing not to be thought of. The fisherman and his wife stood aghast on the doorstep, holding on fast by the doorpost, while the foam splashed over their faces.

"Did I not tell thee that there is no luck in Sunday fishing?" said Matte sulkily; and his wife was so frightened that she never even once thought of Ahti's cows.

As there was nothing to be done, they went in. Their eyes were heavy for lack of slumber, and they slept as soundly as if there had not been such a thing as an angry sea roaring furiously around their lonely dwelling. When they awoke, the sun was high in the

The Storm Raged in Every Direction

heavens, the tempest had ceased, and only the swell of the sea rose in silvery heavings against the red rock.

"What can that be?" said the old woman, as she peeped out of the door.

"It looks like a big seal," said Matte.

"As sure as I live, it's a cow!" exclaimed Maie. And certainly it was a cow, a fine red cow, fat and flourishing, and looking as if it had been fed all its days on spinach. It wandered peacefully up and down the shore, and never so much as even looked at the poor little tufts of grass, as if it despised such fare.

Matte could not believe his eyes, but a cow she seemed, and a cow she was found to be; and when the old woman began to milk her, every pitcher and pan was soon filled with the most delicious milk.

The old man troubled his head in vain as to how she came there, and sallied forth to seek for his lost net. He had not proceeded far when he found it cast up on the shore, and so full of fish that not a mesh was visible.

"It is all very fine to possess a cow," said Matte, as he cleaned the fish; "but what are we going to feed her on?"

"We shall find some means," said his wife; and the cow found the means herself. She went out and cropped the seaweed which grew in great abundance near the shore, and always kept in good condition. Every one, Prince alone excepted, thought she was a clever beast; but Prince barked at her, for he had now got a rival.

"It's a Cow!"

From that day the red rock overflowed with milk and puddings, and every net was filled with fish. Matte and Maie grew fat on this fine living, and daily became richer. She churned quantities of butter, and he hired two men to help him in his fishing. The sea lay before him like a big fish tank, out of which he hauled as many as he required; and the cow continued to fend for herself.

In autumn, when Matte and Maie went ashore, the cow went to sea, and in spring, when they returned to the rock, there she stood awaiting them.

"We shall require a better house," said Maie the following summer; "the old one is too small for ourselves and the men."

"Yes," said Matte. So he built a large cottage, with a real lock to the door, and a store-house for fish as well; and he and his men caught such quantities of fish that they sold tons of salmon, herring, and cod.

"I am quite overworked with so many folk," said Maie; "a girl to help me would not come amiss."

"Get one, then," said her husband; and so they hired a girl.

Then Maie said: "We have too little milk for all these folk. Now that I have a servant, with the same amount of trouble she could look after three cows."

"All right, then," said her husband, somewhat provoked, "you can sing a song to the fairies."

This annoyed Maie, but nevertheless she rowed out to sea on Sunday night and sang as before:

The Old House is Too Small.

Oh, Ahti, with the long, long beard,
    Who dwellest in the deep blue sea,
A thousand cows are in thy herd,
    I pray thee give three unto me.

The following morning, instead of one, three cows stood on the island, and they all ate seaweed and fended for themselves like the first one.

"Art thou satisfied now?" said Matte to his wife.

"I should be quite satisfied," said his wife, "if only I had two servants to help, and if I had some finer clothes. Don't you know that I am addressed as Madam?"

"Well, well," said her husband. So Maie got several servants, and clothes fit for a great lady.

"Everything would now be perfect if only we had a little better dwelling for summer. You might build us a two-story house, and fetch soil to make a garden. Then you might make a little arbor up there to let us have a sea-view; and we might have a fiddler to fiddle to us of an evening, and a little steamer to take us to church in stormy weather," she declared.

"Anything more?" asked Matte; but he did everything that his wife wished. The rock Ahtola became so grand and Maie so great that all the sea-urchins and herring were lost in wonderment. Even Prince was fed on beefsteaks and cream scones till at last he was as round as a butter jar.

Three Cows Stood on the Island.

"Are you satisfied now?" asked Matte.

"I should be quite satisfied," said Maie, "if only I had thirty cows. At least that number is required for such a household."

"Go to the fairies," said Matte.

His wife set out in the new steamer and sang to the Sea King. Next morning thirty cows stood on the shore, all finding food for themselves.

"Know'st thou, good man, that we are far too cramped on this wretched rock, and where am I to find room for so many cows?" asked Maie.

"There is nothing to be done but to pump out the sea," replied Matte.

"Rubbish!" said his wife. "Who can pump out the sea?"

"Try with thy new steamer, there is a pump in it."

Maie knew well that her husband was only making fun of her, but still her mind was set upon the same subject. "I never could pump the sea out," thought she, "but perhaps I might fill it up, if I were to make a big dam. I might heap up sand and stones, and make our island as big again."

Maie loaded her boat with stones and went out to sea. The fiddler was with her, and fiddled so finely that Ahti and Wellamos and all the sea's daughters rose to the surface of the water to listen to the music.

"What is that shining so brightly in the waves?" asked Maie.

"That is sea foam glinting in the sunshine," answered the

All the Sea's Daughters Rose.

fiddler.

"Throw out the stones," said Maie.

The people in the boat began to throw out the stones, splash, splash, right and left, into the foam. One stone hit the nose of Wellamos's chief lady-in-waiting, another scratched the Sea Queen herself on the cheek, a third plumped close to Ahti's head and tore off half of the Sea King's beard; then there was a commotion in the sea, the waves bubbled and bubbled like boiling water in a pot.

"Whence comes this gust of wind?" said Maie; and as she spoke the sea opened and swallowed up the steamer. Maie sank to the bottom like a stone, but, stretching out her arms and legs, she rose to the surface, where she found the fiddler's fiddle, and used it as a float. At the same moment she saw close beside her the terrible head of Ahti, and he had only half a beard!

"Why did you throw stones at me?" roared the Sea King.

"Oh, your majesty, it was a mistake! Put some bear's grease on your beard and that will soon make it grow again."

"Dame, did I not give you all you asked for — nay, even more?"

"Truly, truly, your majesty. Many thanks for the cows."

"Well, where is the gold from the sun and the silver from the moon that you promised me?"

"Ah, your majesty, they have been scattered day and night upon the sea, except when the sky was overcast," answered Maie slyly.

Another Scratched the Sea Queen Herself.

"I'll teach you!" roared the Sea King; and with that he gave the fiddle such a puff that it sent the old woman up like a skyrocket on to her island. There Prince lay, as famished as ever, gnawing the bones of a crow. There sat Matte in his ragged grey jacket, quite alone, on the steps of the old hut, mending a net.

"Heavens, mother," said he, "where are you coming from at such a whirlwind pace, and what makes you in such a dripping condition?"

Maie looked around her amazed, and said, "Where is our two-story house?"

"What house?" asked her husband.

"Our big house, and the flower garden, and the men and the maids, and the thirty beautiful cows, and the steamer, and everything else?"

"You are talking nonsense, mother," said he. "The students have quite turned your head, for you sang silly songs last evening while we were rowing, and then you could not sleep till early morning. We had stormy weather during the night, and when it was past I did not wish to waken you, so rowed out alone to rescue the net."

"But I've seen Ahti," rejoined Maie.

"You've been lying in bed, dreaming foolish fancies, mother, and then in your sleep you walked into the water."

"But there is the fiddle," said Maie.

"A fine fiddle! It is only an old stick. No, no, old woman,

"I'll Teach You!"

another time we will be more careful. Good luck never attends fishing on a Sunday."

Maie looked about her at Ahtola; truly it looked the same as it always had. No sign was there of anything of her greatness: not cows nor servants nor casks overflowing with fish of such miraculous abundance that now seemed to exist only in her visions of them.

Matte was lighting his pipe as she gazed at him; as real as the little red light that glowed from it was her remembrance of all that Ahti had given and then taken away. She brushed her eyes with her hand as if to clear her sight, but all she could see was Prince, frolicking on the bare beach as ever he was wont to do; the same tufts of herbs and reeds as ever; and Matte, looking through narrowed but twinkling eyes at her as the wind whistled around the rock and the old weathercock creaked on the roof.

"Ah well," she thought, "even if it was only a dream, how nice it was to have had all that fresh cream!"

And as she gazed, the sea boiled and bubbled as it had when Ahti had appeared. The foam frothed and gleamed, but the light shining on it was only the reflection of the sun as it lowered itself in the sky before disappearing into the sea.

"Good Luck Never Attends Sunday Fishing."